Did Bigfoot
Steal Christmas?

Other books by Dr. Mary Ellen Erickson

Grandma Mary & Bonbon series: *First Day of School, Snowstorm,* and *Bonbon's Special Christmas.* Children's picture books that teach character-building traits and emphasize rules and work ethics.

Peanut Butter Club Mystery series: *What Happened to the Deer?, Who Jinxed the C&G Ranch?,* and *Did Bigfoot Steal Christmas?.* This series is full of fun and adventure and emphasizes responsibility, friendship, and the special relationship between grandparents and grandchildren.

Common Sense Caregiving: A nonfiction adult book based on research that stresses the positive side of caring for the elderly.

Humble and Homemade: Survival in Tough Times: An adult nonfiction book of short stories, cooking, and gardening that shows you how to make the very best of what you already have.

Otis: An historical-fiction novel that includes humor, romance, mystery, and some complicated family relationships.

Geezettes: Books 1 and **2:** Adult novels about retired women. This series emphasizes humor, romance, and the importance of friendships as we grow older.

Did Bigfoot Steal Christmas?

Peanut Butter Club Mysteries: Book 3

Mary Ellen Erickson, PhD

iUniverse, Inc.
Bloomington

DID BIGFOOT STEAL CHRISTMAS?
Peanut Butter Club Mysteries: Book 3

This is a work of fiction. All of the characters, names, incidents, organizations, and dialogue in this novel are either the products of the author's imagination or are used fictitiously.

iUniverse books may be ordered through booksellers or by contacting:

iUniverse
1663 Liberty Drive
Bloomington, IN 47403
www.iuniverse.com
1-800-Authors (1-800-288-4677)

ISBN: 978-1-4759-9448-3 (sc)
ISBN: 978-1-4759-9450-6 (hc)
ISBN: 978-1-4759-9449-0 (ebk)

Library of Congress Control Number: 2013910826

Printed in the United States of America

iUniverse rev. date: 06/18/2013

Contents

Van skidding into the ditch

Chapter 1

Destination: Husky Hideaway

"Ahhhhhh!" Jenny screamed as the van slid into the ditch. The twelve-year-old, blonde, blue-eyed drama queen always overreacted to any situation.

"You just busted my eardrum!" Audrey, a fourteen-year-old high-school freshman yelled, and she scowled at her cousin.

"Now, now, children, settle down!" Grandma Abby tried to quiet the six youngsters who were all talking at once. She smoothed her short, curly gray hair and started putting on her warm stocking cap. Next she bent over and picked her glasses up off the floor where they had fallen when the van had come to an abrupt halt.

"Grandpa should be able to get out of this ditch if we all get out and push," Grandma assured the children as they became eerily quiet.

"Yeah," Grandpa Josh agreed. "All of you get out while I turn down my hearing aid. This noise has given me a headache."

The three girls piled out of the old van first. Audrey's warm stocking cap was sitting loosely on top of her heavy, shoulder-length auburn hair. She pulled the cap down so low it almost hid her big brown eyes. "It's cold out here," she wailed.

1

Jenny followed her older cousin out of the car. She didn't have any comments, for a change. Missy, Jenny's twelve-year-old friend, was next. Her long black hair, neatly braided, showed from under her warm wool cap, which protruded on either side of her face to protect her sparkling black eyes.

The boys scampered out on the heels of the girls. Denny, Jenny's willowy blond twin brother, was first, followed by his friend Randy, who was a year older and taller. He had dark shoulder-length hair and black eyes that reflected his Native American heritage.

Ty, the youngest member of the family, with his reddish-brown hair, big brown eyes, and freckles, was the last child to exit. He was followed by Laddie, the ageing family collie.

"This is so exciting," the eight-year-old bubbled. "I love pushing cars."

"How do you know you love pushing cars?" Denny asked. "How many cars have you pushed out of ditches? Pinhead!"

"Don't be sarcastic, Denny," Grandma scolded. "We need cooperation here—not criticism."

"Come on, Denny, we'll push from the front," Randy suggested. "It's probably best to go backward to get out of this ditch."

"Randy's right," Grandma said, smiling at their thirteen-year-old guest. "Now, all of you line up at the front of the car."

"Randy's always right." Denny grinned at his friend. "He knows lots of stuff about lots of things."

"Yeah, sure," Audrey scoffed. "He's a regular walking encyclopedia."

I'm glad he's here to help me with all these dumb girls, Denny thought.

Grandma shook her head in dismay, took a deep breath, and let out a puff of air. "It has been a long day! I'm sure the ski lodge is just around the corner. Let's all cool it another few minutes, and then we'll be able to relax. Cousin Hannah promised us a lovely pork dinner when we called her about an hour ago."

"Get in front of the van and push," Grandpa ordered the group from his open window. "When I put the van into reverse, everyone push at once."

The six children lined up in the snow at the front of the van, while Laddie went across the road to potty. Audrey had to push aside a small bush to find a place to stand. Grandma grabbed the rearview mirror and door handle on the passenger side of the van. When Grandpa put the van into reverse and pushed down the gas pedal, the van began moving backward.

"Push!" Jenny cried, as she pushed with all her might. She had appointed herself cheerleader.

Everyone pushed as hard as they could, and the van was soon back on the road.

"Hurrah!" The children jumped and cheered.

When the celebrating ended, the group heard Laddie barking. The family pet seemed to be focused on something in the woods.

"What's that smelly dog barking at?" Jenny asked.

"I thought I saw something moving out there," Audrey said.

"I didn't see anything," Ty said.

"Me either," Denny agreed.

"Well, we don't have time to run after something in the woods, so get into the van," Grandpa shouted out the window. "It's beginning to snow. Let's get to the lodge before dark, or we'll really be in a mess."

I know I saw something—sort of big and furry, Audrey thought as she settled down in her seat for the remainder of the trip to the lodge.

*   *   *

The Haskell grandparents, their four grandchildren, and two of their neighbors' grandchildren had been on the road since early morning. They were traveling from their small diversified farm north of Aberdeen, South Dakota, to a small, cross-country ski lodge in Northwestern Minnesota.

The Lake Toby Resort was well known in the Marshall County region for its cross-country skiing and dogsled racing in the winter and its water skiing and walleye fishing in the summer. Since the Husky Hideaway Lodge on Lake Toby was also a bed and breakfast, which featured Hannah's excellent cooking, in the fall of the year many hunters came to the lodge to hunt pheasants, ducks, and deer.

Basil and Hannah (Larson) Elliott had purchased the lodge after they'd retired from their office jobs in East Grand Forks, Minnesota, in 2000. Hannah had been an outstanding cross-country skier at the University of Minnesota during the 1960s and Basil was interested in raising husky sled dogs, so the lodge was the perfect place for them to practice their hobbies and keep busy in their retirement years.

The Elliotts had invited the Haskells and their grandchildren to the lodge for the Christmas holiday. Not many guests came during the holiday, so there were plenty of rooms available.

The Elliotts' only son, Brad, was an engineer who worked for a large company in South Africa. He didn't come home very often. Hannah and Basil thought it would be fun to have a bunch of kids around for the holidays.

* * *

"That must be Lake Toby," Grandma Abby said, pointing to a large frozen body of water on the right side of the road, while the old van moved slowly up the hill toward a large, Tudor-style two-story building.

"At last we're here!" Jenny said, and she gave a big sigh of relief.

"I'm hungry!" Denny complained.

Grandpa stopped the van in front of the lodge. The children piled out as if the van were on fire and ran up the porch steps to the ornately decorated entrance to the lodge. The Christmas wreath hanging on the door had a sign beneath it that read *Velcommen,* the Scandinavian word for welcome.

Hannah flung the doors wide open before the children had a chance to ring the bell. "Come in," she shouted above the clamor of excitement.

The sixty-five-year-old, tall, muscular woman picked Audrey up from the floor of the porch as she hugged her. Hannah's long, gray-blonde hair was tied in a bun at the nape of her neck, and her blue eyes sparkled when she saw the children.

Next Hannah hugged Jenny and then Denny. After tossing Ty into the air, she gave him a big bear hug that left the youngster breathless.

"And who are these two strangers?" Hannah asked, looking at Randy and Missy.

"This is Missy, and that's Randy." Jenny introduced her friends by pointing at them. "They are Grandma and Grandpa's neighbors' grandkids."

"I hope you don't mind us bring them along?" Grandma asked as she approached the door.

"Not at all. The more the merrier." Hannah laughed loudly with joy.

Just then, Hannah's husband, Basil, appeared at the door. "Welcome," he said as he broke loose with a robust laugh that sounded like Santa Claus.

Basil was a dark French Canadian. His black beard was showing signs of gray, and the graying black hair on his head was thinning. Basil was also muscular, with sparkling dark eyes. He stood well over six foot four inches tall.

The children became quiet while they stared at the Paul Bunyan lookalike from the north woods. Paul Bunyan was a giant fictitious hero of folklore they'd heard of who had great skill in harvesting lumber from the Northeastern United States forests.

Grandpa Josh walked over to Basil and shook his hand. "Do you know what you've gotten yourself into?" he asked Basil.

Basil let out a big *ho, ho, ho* chuckle that shook the porch. Then he answered, "This looks like a lively group. Hope they can chop wood!"

"Chop wood!" the children exclaimed together.

"Sure," Basil said with a wink. "All we burn here is wood. We need lots of chopped wood to keep the fires going. You want to be warm, don't you?"

"Well, yes," Audrey answered first. "We can help, can't we?" She looked at her fellow travelers.

They all nodded meekly in agreement. No one felt the need to argue with Basil.

"We're okay for tonight." Basil smiled. "No chores until morning; then we'll all learn how to chop wood and feed dogs."

"Dogs? Oh boy!" Ty said excitedly. "How many dogs?"

"About a dozen Siberian huskies. This is the Husky Hideaway, you know," Basil said proudly.

"Bring in all your things," Hannah instructed. "We'd better close this door soon, or we'll have to chop more wood before the night is over."

Everyone marched quickly to the van and grabbed their suitcases, along with boxes full of food, Christmas gifts, and warm clothes. Grandma had spent days packing her canned goodies, lots of warm boots, mittens, coats, and gifts for everyone—she was always well organized. In case of a snowstorm, they would be well equipped through the holidays.

Chapter 2

Who is Sasquatch?

The conversation around the big oak table in the kitchen was very lively. The children were all excited and had many questions about the Husky Hideaway.

"How often do you go to dogsled races?" Denny mumbled through a mouthful of potatoes and gravy.

"Don't talk with your mouth full of food," Grandma Abby scolded. Then she added with a sigh, "Children—I don't know how many times I have to tell them!"

Cousin Basil laughed. "Well, young man, I'll tell you. We go whenever we feel the dogs are ready and can win a race. You have to pay entrance fees, so it gets costly if you never win. We won't be entering any races until after Christmas."

"How many dogs to a sled?" Randy asked while chewing on a piece of pork roast.

"Depends on the race, conditions of the course, health of the animals—stuff like that. I only have nine racing dogs right now, so that's all I can use. Two of my female dogs are with pups right now, so they don't race. I usually go with seven dogs."

"You mean there are pups here?" Ty gasped with so much excitement that he nearly tipped his glass of milk as he reached for another swallow to wash down his food. He was eating so fast that he seemed to have forgotten how to chew properly.

"Slow down, young man!" Grandpa warned. "You'll choke on your food."

"Yes," Basil said in reply to Ty's question, "we've got two sets of pups—eight in all."

"Can we go see them, please?" Ty begged.

"No," the four adults answered in unison.

"They're bedded down for the night. We'll see them in the morning," Basil promised.

"How many different kinds of huskies are there?" Audrey asked. She always wanted to be the one to ask the most intelligent questions.

"The two most popular purebred sled dogs are the Siberian husky and the Alaskan Malamute," Basil replied. Then he went on to explain. "There are many types of mongrel dogs used in teams too. Back in the late 1980s, a team of standard poodles ran in the Iditarod and did okay."

"What is the Iditarod?" Ty asked.

"The Iditarod is an annual sled-dog race that lasts for eight to fourteen days over a thousand-mile stretch from Anchorage to Nome, Alaska. It's very popular in Alaska," Basil explained.

"I'll bet that it takes a really tough guy with strong dogs to win that race," Randy speculated.

"Not at all!" Hannah grinned. "The race has been won many times by women, and the dogs are male and female."

"Oh," Randy muttered while digging in to his green beans. The girls at the table snickered.

"What kind of huskies do you raise?" Denny asked.

"We have the Siberian huskies, because we like to sell them for breeding stock and racers. However, I've seen some mixed breeds that are very good racers."

"This all sounds very exciting," Jenny commented. "I can't wait to see a race."

"Don't you have any questions?" Hannah asked Missy.

Missy smiled shyly. "No, I learn more when I'm listening."

Everyone laughed.

"Ain't that the truth?" Hannah exclaimed. "Now, who needs dessert?"

"I do!" the children all shouted at once.

Grandpa Josh turned down his hearing aid and shook his head.

"What's for dessert?" Ty asked.

"Gooseberry pie," Hannah answered.

"Gooseberry!" Ty gasped in horror. "How many geese did you have to kill to find enough berries to make a pie?"

Everyone laughed.

"None at all," Hannah said. "Gooseberries grow on small bushes. We grow the Pixwell brand. They turn a pale pink when they are ripe and make excellent pies and preserves. I sell the pies and jams to tourists and guests in the summer."

"Here you go," she said as she handed Ty a piece of pie with a scoop of vanilla ice cream.

"Ty looked at the pie, lowered his head, and said, "I think I'll wait for everyone else to get their pie before I eat mine."

"He's chicken," Denny said. "He's afraid to go first."

"Okay, young man," Hannah said as she handed Denny a big piece of pie and ice cream. "You go first."

Denny stared at the pie.

"Give it to me," Missy said, "I like gooseberry pie. I've tasted it many times at my Aunt Red Feather's place—it's delicious."

Missy took a big slice of the pie with some ice cream, and began eating. "Mmmm," she said as she tasted the heavenly dessert.

Ty dug into his pie. He couldn't let a girl be braver than he was. Soon everyone was enjoying Hannah's wonderful dessert.

* * *

After supper, the family sat around the fireplace in the large family room, which they called the great room. The logs crackled as they burned. Once in a while sparks shot out onto the hearth.

"I think I saw something in the woods when we slid into the ditch," Audrey said. "Laddie was barking, and I swear I saw some large, hairy beast run through the trees."

"Just like a girl," Randy said as he shook his head. "They are always afraid of everything that moves in the woods."

"Well," Basil said, looking concerned, "we've had sightings of Sasquatch lately."

"Who's Sasquatch?" Jenny asked, wrinkling her brow while she made a funny face.

"Sasquatch is also called Bigfoot, Yeti, or the Abominable Snowman, depending on who sees it and where it is spotted," Hannah explained. "I've never seen it, but people claim it's a big hair-covered creature that looks something like an ape. I think it's all a hoax."

"I've heard of such a creature," Audrey said. "It's probably some big person dressed in an ape suit."

"That could be true," Basil agreed, "but why would anyone want to go to all that trouble just to scare someone?"

"People do strange things," Grandma Abby suggested. "I guess they need to get a life."

"Amen to that!" Hannah ended the conversation when she saw the fear in Ty's eyes. *No use scaring the children,* she thought.

* * *

The children got to sleep in the hunters' dorm attached to the back of the lodge. They got to this by going through the small shed that was attached to the kitchen. The two large rooms in the dorm were paneled with knotty pine and had a large picture window at one end and a very large closet at the other end. The four beds in each room were made of maple wood and were very comfortable, with pillow-soft mattresses. Each bed had a small dresser to put clothes and other items into. Each room had a small refrigerator, and there was a big colorful braided rug in the middle of each room. There was also a bathroom for each large room. The whole look was warm and comfortable.

"Wow—four beds!" Ty said excitedly as they entered the boy's dorm room. "Now Laddie can have his own bed." The old collie followed Ty everywhere and was his best buddy.

"Whoopee ding!" Denny said with a smirk. "It's not enough we have to put up with the squirt—we also have to take the old dog."

"Relax!" Randy patted his buddy on the back. "These are pretty cool digs we are in."

"Yeah, this is a nice room," Denny agreed. "I guess we can handle the two oddballs." Then he playfully poked Ty with his fist.

Ty ignored the poke and picked out two beds on the right side of the room. He threw his suitcase on one of the beds. "You take that other bed, Laddie." He pointed to the empty bed.

The old dog looked at Ty and then at the bed Ty was pointing to. Next he jumped onto the bed with the suitcase on it.

"Guess you have a sleeping partner." Randy laughed.

"Maybe that's good," Ty said. "It could get cold out here."

"Maybe," Randy said with a nod. He started unpacking his clothes and hung them up on hangers in the closet.

* * *

Husky Hideaway

"Wake up!" Audrey shook Jenny, who was snuggled under her quilt. "It snowed all night, and it's absolutely gorgeous outside. Come look out the window and see!"

"Go away!" Jenny snarled.

"Sleep if you like!" Audrey shook her head in disgust. "I'm going to see if I can help Grandma and Hannah with breakfast, after I go outside to check out this beautiful scene."

The door to the room shut quietly as Audrey headed for the kitchen shed. She was dressed in her warm long underwear, bright-red ski sweater, blue jeans, and snow boots. Before she went into the kitchen, she went out the back door to survey the winter wonderland around her.

The lodge was built close to the shore of Lake Toby. Most of the lake was covered with snow, but there were some spots where the snow had blown off the frozen ice.

Great spot to go skating, Audrey thought. Then she shivered. *I'll have to have more clothes on than this if I want to go outside today.*

She hurried back inside to the kitchen, where a fire in the old wood-burning cook stove was crackling and everything was warm and toasty. Grandma and Hannah were busy making scrambled eggs and French toast—Audrey's favorites.

"That smells so-o-o-o good," Audrey purred. She looked around. "Were are Grandpa and Basil?"

"Clearing away the snow so they can get out to the woodshed and dog barn," Hannah answered.

"Oh." Audrey said as she walked over to the table. "Should I set the table?" she asked.

"Please do." Hannah smiled. "The dishes and flatware are over there." She pointed to some cupboards next to the table.

Audrey was busy setting the table when she heard Basil and Grandpa stomping in the shed next to the kitchen. She also heard them talking softly. She went to the shed door and opened it slightly, so she could peek through and listen.

"Why do you think some of the wood was scattered in the yard, Josh?" Basil asked.

"Don't know. Not much wind last night—couldn't have blown the wood off the piles," Josh answered.

"That's what I was thinking too," Basil agreed. "Couldn't have been wild animals. They usually don't bother woodpiles. We do get some wild animals around here in the winter—mostly wolves. Some come right up to the dog barns when they smell the dogs or hear them barking."

"I didn't hear any dogs bark last night," Josh said. "I didn't see any tracks either, but the drifting of the snow could have covered any tracks by morning."

"Me neither," Basil agreed. "Whatever or whoever it was must have been human. My dogs are used to people. They don't bark much when people are around."

The men brushed the snow off their coats and boots. They noticed Audrey peeking through the door, so they stopped talking to each other to greet her.

"Well, look who's up bright and early," Basil said with a chuckle.

"She's usually the first one up of the bunch," Grandpa said.

"Good morning," Audrey said in a bubbly voice as she opened the door for the men to come into the toasty, warm kitchen with their armloads of wood for the stove. *Hmm,* she thought, *it looks like there might be a mystery here to solve. First we have a strange creature in the woods; then we have something scattering wood around the yard. I'll have to call a meeting of the Peanut Butter Club.*

Chapter 3

Lots of Work and Fun

"I can't wait to see the puppies," Ty proclaimed as he pulled on his snow boots. Grandma had insisted they all put on coats, mittens, snow pants, and boots before going out to the dog barn.

The six youngsters raced through the knee-high snow to the dog barn. This long one-story shed had a low ceiling. It had seen better days. Basil had fixed up the barn when he and Hannah had purchased the Husky Hideaway ten years ago. The barn was long, low, and inexpensive looking. It had a covered entranceway and one large window toward the front, on the south side. Smoke was floating slowly into the air out of the smoke pipe on the roof.

The dogs inside the barn heard the children coming and began to bark. Ty burst through the door first, to a chorus of wild barking. He stopped abruptly—not sure of where to go next. The barking grew louder.

The dogs each had their own pen. The wooden fences around each pen kept the dogs separated.

As each of the young people came through the door, they stopped in wonder. Looking at all the beautiful dogs barking and jumping in their pens, the children were fearful and amazed.

The barking got louder.

Basil walked through the door, followed by Grandpa, and they stood amidst the bewildered youngsters. "Hush!" Basil shouted to the dogs. It became instantly quiet.

"I wish that would work with the kids," Grandpa said with a laugh.

Basil was carrying a big pail of meat scraps, and Grandpa was carrying a bag of dog food. The supplies to feed the dogs were stored in the shed off the kitchen.

Basil handed the pail of meat scraps to Denny and Randy. "Here, you give each dog three of these scraps in their food dish."

Next, he gave Audrey, Jenny, and Missy the bag of dog food, along with a big cup. "Give each dog a large cupful of this food," he instructed.

Then Basil looked at Ty; he was hugging Laddie to protect him from the other dogs, who were giving him a good looking-over. "You and Laddie follow the feeders with a treat," Basil instructed Ty as he handed the young boy a big box full of dog treats from a high shelf in the barn. "Josh and I will get water from the house to fill the water dishes."

Basil and Josh left the barn with two large pails, leaving the children standing in a group, looking at each other and their dog food.

"How wild are these dogs?" Denny asked.

"We'll have to go into the pens to find out," Randy answered.

"You go first," Denny said.

"Okay, give me a piece of meat, and I'll open the door and go inside." Randy pretended to be brave, but the look on his face said he wasn't too sure about what he was doing.

"Good luck!" Jenny said with sympathy. She didn't want to see Randy attacked by a husky. Then she added, "His name is Buster—it says so on this gate plaque. He sure is beautiful," she mumbled while staring at the large, male, Siberian husky.

Buster was black and white, with gray showing where the black and white met. The black covered most of his upper body and tail as well as the outside of his ears. A black strip that circled his eyes also ran down the top of his white snout. It looked like he was wearing a mask. His lower body and belly, four feet, and a small splotch above each eye were white. There were other white splotches on his throat, neck, and tail. The most outstanding feature was his ice-blue eyes.

Buster standing at attention

Buster stood at attention when Randy entered the pen. "Nice, Buster," Randy said softly as he walked up to the large dog and petted his head. Then he held the scrap of meat up in front of Buster's face. The dog grabbed the meat and gobbled it down. "Good boy," Randy said, petting the dog on the head and scratching him behind his ears. "Come on in, Denny; he's nice and tame."

Denny entered the pen with two more scraps of meat and fed the big dog. The boys talked to the husky and gave him a big hug. "Our turn now," Audrey said. "You feed the others, and we'll follow." She wasn't too keen about being the first one in the pens.

Missy went into the pen first and petted Buster on his head; then she sat down beside him and whispered in his ear, "Nice dog; you're beautiful! Want to be my friend?"

Buster licked Missy's face. She smiled.

Audrey and Jenny put a big cupful of dog food into the bowl on the floor and then gave Buster hugs and kisses. Buster seemed more interested in eating his food than being friendly, so the girls moved to the next pen.

Ty waited until Buster was done with all his food before he entered the pen. "Want a treat?" Ty asked.

Buster was licking his lips with his long tongue. *Is he thinking that I might make a delicious meal?* Ty wondered.

As Buster walked toward Ty, Ty panicked. "Sit down!" Ty ordered the dog. Buster sat down and put up his right paw.

"Wow!" Ty exclaimed. "He can do tricks." Ty fed Buster a treat and was about to sit down to play with the husky when he heard Audrey scream, "Puppies!"

Ty whirled around and ran to the back of the barn, where the rest of the gang had gathered and were staring into a pen that was occupied by a beautiful female husky named Babe. She had the same fur design on her body and face as Buster did, but her colors were white, cream, and shades of brown. She had four puppies with her. Two were cream, brown, and white, like their mother, and the other two had the same colors and markings as Buster. All of the puppies had the same ice-blue eyes as their mother and Buster.

Babe's puppies

"Looks like Buster might be the big daddy of these puppies," Randy said with a grin.

"Sure does." Denny smiled at his buddy in an all-knowing way.

"Most of these huskies look like Buster," Jenny said. "He might be the father of them all. We'll have to ask Basil."

"Look over here!" Ty said excitedly. "More puppies!"

The children gathered around the gate of a pen where a young black-and-white female was feeding four very young puppies. There was a small electric heater mounted on the wall near the pen to keep the young puppies warm.

"Those pups look different." Audrey looked surprised.

"They sure do!" Jenny exclaimed. "Two of them are all black, and the other two have very little white—just feet and snout, and a splotch over each eye."

"That's Delilah and her pups," Basil said as he walked up behind the children. "She's a bit of a naughty girl on occasion—she runs away from home. I'm afraid those pups aren't Buster's. They probably belong to Chico, the head of the wolf pack that hangs around here in the woods. I won't be able to sell them as purebreds, but they'll make very good sled dogs."

"Did you hear that?" Denny whispered to Randy. "There are wolf packs around here."

"Yeah, I know," Randy whispered back. "I heard them last night."

"Sure hope I never run into any!" Denny said and he shivered.

"Piece of cake." Randy grinned. "I know how to handle wolves."

"Yeah, sure." Denny poked his friend on the arm. "Let's feed the rest of these dogs."

* * *

"Who wants to play with some of the dogs outside?" Basil asked when the dogs had all been fed and watered.

"I do!" All the children shouted and waved their hands at once. Basil released six of his tamest, most well-mannered adult dogs, giving one to each youngster to lead outside.

Then the fun began. The children ran, laughed, screamed, rolled, and slid as they played ice tag with the huskies on Lake Toby. The dogs ran after the children and jumped on their backs when they caught up with one of them. Basil and Josh oversaw the fun to make sure things didn't get too rough. The dogs obeyed Basil. If they got too rough, he'd make them sit at attention at the side of the ice for a while. Basil was really good with the huskies. They understood his every command.

After the children and dogs were all exhausted from playing ice tag, Basil put the dogs back into the barn, while instructing the children to meet him behind the dog barn by the woodpiles.

"Time to pick up the wood scattered all over the yard and into the woods," Basil announced when they were all gathered behind the barn.

"Why is there wood everywhere?" Jenny asked, looking around in surprise.

"Because someone scattered it everywhere," Grandpa told her.

"How do you know it was someone?" Audrey asked.

"Because there wasn't enough wind to blow it around, and also, the scattered wood seems to lead to woods. I think someone was trying to steal wood, then got frightened, and dropped it along the way as he made his escape."

"Why couldn't it have been an animal?" Denny asked.

"Animals don't very often steal wood." Basil chuckled.

"Let's hurry and pick this all up so we can go inside and warm up," Audrey suggested as she dug a large chunk of wood out of the snow. Then she added, "We can solve this mystery later."

All five of her peers looked at her—they knew exactly what she meant.

Chapter 4

Chopping Wood

Chopping wood was not an easy task. After lunch, Basil took all the children out behind the dog barns where the blocks of wood were stacked. These blocks, or logs, as they were called, had been cut from dead trees several years ago. They were all dried and cured to make for easier chopping.

Basil picked up a block of wood about one and a half feet high and twelve inches in diameter and set the block up on its end on a wooden stand made from an old tree trunk. The stand was about two feet tall and three feet in diameter. Next, he picked up a very sharp ax. Basil had a chain with a bungee cord on it, hanging from his arm. He placed the chain and cord around the bottom of the wood block. "This will keep the wood from flying all over the place when I chop the block," Basil explained.

Basil picked up the ax, raised it over his head, and brought it down with a mighty blow in the center of the wood block. The block cracked down the middle. Then he chopped around in a circle on top of the block, as if cutting a pie. Each quick chop was about three inches from the previous chop. The wood cracked as he worked his way around the top of the block.

Basil picked up the whole block of chopped wood and handed it to Denny. "Take this into the dog barn, and stack it on the pile of chopped wood. Make sure the pieces come apart," he instructed as he removed the chain and bungee cord.

After Denny had taken off with the wood, Basil asked, "Who would like to try this?"

"I would!" all the children shouted at once.

"Okay, you go first, Randy," Basil said as he handed the teenager the ax.

Missy brought a block of wood from the pile and set it up on the tree-trunk stand. Audrey and Jenny put the chain and bungee cord around the bottom of the log.

"Everyone back up!" Grandpa ordered. He thought Randy might miss the block of wood or do something else that would cause the log or ax to hit someone.

Randy raised the ax above his head and brought it down with all his strength. The ax stuck in the middle of the block. Everyone stood silent as Basil walked over to the block and started pulling the ax out.

"It's okay," he said to Randy. "Not many of us ever split a block of wood on the first try." Basil handed the ax back to Randy and said, "Try again. Come down in the same spot if possible."

Randy raised the ax, aimed carefully, and struck again. This time the block cracked down the middle. Everyone cheered.

"Good work, Randy," Basil said. "Now, chop around the outer edge of the circle as if you were cutting a pie into about eight pieces. These blows don't have to be as hard, but they need to be accurate."

When Randy had finished the log, he picked it up and raised it above his head in a show of victory.

Everyone shouted, "Hurrah for Randy!"

"Who's next?" Basil asked.

Grandpa said, "I think Audrey and Randy should try to do the chopping, and Missy and Jenny can put the blocks on the stand. Ty and Denny can haul them away into the barn." He was afraid the younger children wouldn't be able to handle the ax and would hurt themselves.

"I think you're right, Josh," Basil agreed, and then he added, "Josh and I will supervise to make sure no one gets hurt."

Audrey had to try three times before her block of wood cracked in the middle. The chopping process was harder for Audrey because she didn't have the physical strength that Randy had.

Randy watched Audrey, with a big grin on his face. *Girls always think they can do everything that boys can,* he thought. *I guess I showed her.*

Randy and Audrey took turns. After chopping four logs each, the teenagers seemed to be tiring, so Basil said, "That will be enough for today. You kids can go play."

"Yeah!" the children shouted, jumping up and down.

"Can we play ice tag with the rest of the dogs?" Missy asked shyly.

"Sure," Basil answered. "Come into the barn, and I'll give you each a dog."

* * *

That evening, after a supper of fried chicken, baked potatoes, mushroom gravy, fresh rolls, and baked apples, the children got to watch TV. They also were allowed to play computer games. The girls watched a TV program while the boys played computer games.

A little later, "Time for bed," Grandma announced.

Good, Audrey thought. *We need to have a Peanut Butter Club meeting and make plans to solve the Bigfoot mystery.*

"We can meet in our room," Audrey said as the group entered the hunters' dorm. "Let's do that before we get ready for bed."

Peanut Butter Club meeting

"I'll be there after I turn up the electric heater in our room," Randy said. "It's cold in here."

"Don't turn it up too high," Audrey warned. "It's not good to sleep where it's too warm. The air will get too dry and—"

"Yak, yak," Randy said teasingly to Audrey. "Girls are always trying to tell guys what to do. You regulate your room temperature, and we'll regulate ours—okay?"

"Whatever!" Audrey opened the door to the girl's room and went inside. *He's so touchy lately,* she thought.

A few minutes later, the gang was all seated on the floor in the girl's room on the large colorful rug.

"Where's Laddie?" Missy asked.

"He wanted to stay on the nice, warm bed," Ty answered. "I guess he's not interested in Bigfoot. I did invite him."

"Like he knows what an invitation is," Jenny said with a smirk on her face.

"Let's get started," Audrey said in her stern voice. She was getting weary of the bickering.

The kids did the hand sign and pledge before they started. They each held up their right hand and made a fist with their thumb between the middle and first finger. Then they said their pledge: "I promise to follow the clubs rules and keep the club secrets or I'll get kicked out by the other members." After the pledge, they brought their fists down over their hearts to seal the pledge.

Audrey had appointed herself the chairwomen of the group, so she started the meeting.

"Who thinks there is a mystery here?" she asked.

Everyone raised a hand.

"Good. Now, what do we do about it?"

"Let's organize some search parties to find clues," Randy suggested. "The adults would not like all of us running around at once. If we are a little sneaky about what we do, they won't get suspicious."

"Good," Audrey agreed. "You and Denny can go first. You'll need to ask permission to go into the woods. We don't want to get into trouble. You two can start tomorrow, after we finish our chores. You could start at that place in the road where we went into the ditch. I swear I saw something there."

"I suppose we'll have to walk," Denny moaned.

"It won't kill you!" Jenny said in disgust.

"Wait until it's your turn to walk a few miles!" Denny shot back.

"You could learn to cross-country ski," Audrey suggested. "Cousin Hannah is an expert at that, and I'll bet she'd teach us if we asked."

"That would be fun," Missy said excitedly. She very seldom gave an opinion, so everyone looked at her in surprise.

"That sounds like a lot of work!" Jenny complained.

"Oh, for goodness' sake!" Audrey scolded Jenny. "Don't you ever want to learn something new?"

"Not if it's a lot of work!" Jenny shot back.

"Whatever!" Audrey was tired of arguing. "I'm going to learn to ski. It's one way to get around in this country when there is so much snow."

"So what do we do when we get to the ditch we slid into?" Randy asked.

"Well, I was thinking, if that creature was watching us, he may be around there every day, looking for cars coming and going. Maybe he left some tracks. Follow them and see where they lead," Audrey suggested.

"Sounds good," Randy agreed.

"Then it's settled," Audrey said. "Tomorrow, you and Denny see if you can find where this creature lives."

It got quiet in the room.

"I'm scared," Ty said softly. "What if Bigfoot likes to eat little boys?"

"Good!" Denny smiled.

"You're mean, Denny," Missy said as she put her arms around Ty.

"We'll let you and Laddie be our home spies," Audrey said, looking at Ty with sympathy. She knew her little brother wanted to be part of the team, but he was too young to be out running around in the woods. "You can keep an eye on things going on around here. I'm sure that will keep you busy. You can report each night on what you saw and heard, okay?"

"Okay!" Ty grinned and his whole face lit up. "Laddie will like that. He's good at sniffing things out. We'll find lots of clues."

Denny shook his head but didn't say a word. *It must be nice to have so much faith in that old dog,* he thought.

"That it?" Jenny asked.

Audrey looked around. Nobody objected. "This meeting is adjourned," she said. "We'll meet here tomorrow night at the same time—group hug before we go."

The group stood up and formed a circle with their arms around each other, and then Audrey said, "One for all and all for one!"

"What does that mean?" Jenny asked.

Audrey answered in her usual know-it-all fashion. "That's an Alexandre Dumas quote from *The Three Musketeers* book, and it means we should all help one person if they're in trouble, and that one person has to help the entire group."

"That's neat!" Denny smiled.

"Yeah, cool!" Randy said, giving Denny a high five as they exited the room to go to bed.

Snowmobile by the dog barn

Chapter 5

Snowmobile Fun

"Wow," Denny said excitedly as he and Randy exited the kitchen shed and saw the snowmobile sitting in front of the dog barn. The boys had finished their breakfast before the others and decided to go outside to the barn to start feeding and watering the huskies.

"I wonder if it runs." Randy said. He and Denny started racing to see who could get to the snowmobile first.

"It must run," Denny said breathlessly. "How else could it have gotten out here?"

"Well, maybe it was pushed." Randy walked around the machine and examined it carefully.

"Have you ever driven one of these?" Denny asked.

"Sure, Grandpa Elmer owns one. It's old, so it's always breaking down and hard to start. This one looks a little newer."

Basil and Grandpa Josh came out of the shed and were walking toward the barn when they noticed the boys examining the snowmobile.

"How do you like her?" Basil shouted.

"She looks great!" Randy answered. "How old is she?"

"About ten years, I guess. I bought her secondhand several years ago."

"Can we ride her?" Denny asked.

"Sure," Basil replied. "Just as soon as we get the chores done."

"Let's get started," Randy suggested as he headed to the entrance of the dog barn. *I wish those poky girls would hurry up,* he thought.

The dogs barked gleefully as the boys entered the barn. The animals were excited about getting fed and going out to play.

By the time the boys had finished feeding meat scraps to half the dogs, the girls were in the barn, putting dog food into one bowl and giving each dog some water in another bowl. The group had perfected their feeding routine. It didn't take long to get the job done.

*   *   *

"Could I stay and play with Babe's puppies for a while," Ty asked when he'd finished his dog-feeding and wood-chopping chores.

"I guess so," Basil answered. "I'll take Babe out to get some exercise, and she won't bother you. It's good to play with puppies that size. They need to know people are their friends, so they won't be frightened when we start training them in a few more months."

Ty went into the pen as Babe came out. He sat down on the straw-covered cement floor, and soon the puppies were crawling all over him. They wanted to be petted and picked up. Ty giggled and rolled in the straw with the little huskies yipping their puppy "work" sounds.

Denny and Randy were outside with Basil, trying to get the snowmobile started.

"I don't know what's wrong," Basil complained. "It started earlier this morning when I got it out of the garage. Maybe it's gotten cold sitting here for a couple hours."

"Can we push it back into the garage to warm up?" Denny asked.

"Okay, let's try," Basil said. "You take hold of the handlebar and push on that side, and Randy, you take the other side and push. I'll push on the back."

Denny put the machine in neutral, and everyone began pushing at once. The snowmobile glided easily over the packed-down snow path Basil had made earlier that morning. Soon it was sitting in the warm garage that was attached to the house.

"We'll plug it into the electrical outlet, and it will soon be warmed up," Basil said. "In the meantime, let's go exercise the dogs."

* * *

"Who wants a ride?" Randy shouted over the roar of the snowmobile motor. "This isn't the quietest machine, but we got it running," he said proudly while seated in the driver's seat.

After getting the machine started, Randy and Denny had taken it for a spin around the lake. Now they wanted to give others a ride and share the fun.

"I'll take a ride," Jenny said, hopping on behind Denny. It was a bit crowded, but warmer, with three people huddled together on one big seat.

The cold wind bit their faces as they drove swiftly over the frozen lake, occasionally hitting a snowdrift. The machine would bounce over the drift and come down with a thump, causing the snow to fly wildly everywhere. Jenny would scream with delight and bury her face in Denny's back, while hanging on for dear life.

Randy and Denny would laugh and drive faster every time Jenny screamed. The snowmobile flew higher and bounced harder with each snowdrift they hit.

When the boys returned Jenny safely to where the others were standing, Jenny jumped off the machine.

"They drive like crazy," Jenny said with glee. She loved the excitement.

Basil gave the boys a stern look. He did not share Jenny's glee. "You'll have to be careful and drive slower when you have passengers. They might fall off and get hurt," Basil said in a stern warning.

"Yes, sir," Randy and Denny answered in unison. They respected Basil's opinion. They didn't want to lose their driving privileges.

"Who's next?" Basil asked.

"I'll go," Missy volunteered.

"You can sit in the middle," Randy offered. "That way you're not as likely to fall off."

Denny moved back and Missy squeezed between the two boys on the seat. Away they went.

Since they didn't want Missy to complain when her ride was over and get them into more trouble, they drove slowly and carefully.

"That was fun," Missy bubbled when she got off the machine at the starting point. "I'd like to go again sometime," she said shyly.

"I want to drive myself, please," Audrey announced, looking at Basil.

"Okay, young lady." Basil smiled.

Audrey got on the machine, and Basil showed her how to shift, use the throttle, and steer.

"I think I can handle it," Audrey said with a confident smile. "I've driven a four wheeler, and this seems similar."

Audrey looked at Ty. "Want to come along?" she asked.

Ty grinned from ear to ear. "What about Laddie," he asked. "Can he come too?"

"Laddie can go too," Audrey replied. "Put him in the middle, and hold on to him."

Laddie jumped onto the snowmobile seat. He was always ready to go for a ride. Ty wrapped his arms around the old collie and grabbed hold of Audrey's coat. Away they went.

Audrey drove slowly. She didn't want to dump her little brother or hurt the old collie. They drove along the edge of the lake, over the snow drifts, looking at the lovely forest of pine trees covered with snow that sparkled like diamonds in the midday sun.

Audrey scanned the thick forest for signs of something big and furry that was moving. She was hoping to see Bigfoot, a deer, or something else of interest. She didn't see a thing except more pine trees and more snow.

When the three slow riders returned, Basil suggested they go inside to warm up before lunch.

*   *   *

"Do you think we could go for a ride in the forest after lunch and look for animals?" Randy asked before taking a big bite of his chicken-salad sandwich.

"Maybe, for just a short distance," Basil answered. Then he took a big gulp of his milk and added, "That old snowmobile isn't that dependable. I'd hate to see you guys get stalled."

"You boys be home by four—it starts to get dark about five. I don't want you out in the forest after dark," Grandma Abby said with a worried look on her face.

"We'll be fine—don't worry," Denny assured his grandmother.

"I've heard that line before," Grandma said with a weary smile.

Then she turned to the girls and Ty. "The rest of you can help bake cookies and decorate them. Hannah likes help with the Christmas baking. We'll also have to get out the decorations for the tree—after you all go cut one down in the forest. We can decorate the tree when we are all here after supper tonight. It is December twenty-fourth tomorrow—Christmas Eve."

After the boys were bundled up and ready to go, Hannah handed them each a wrapped gingerbread-man cookie. "Just in case you get hungry," she said with a wink as the boys exited the shed door.

* * *

The boys reached the point along the side of the road where Audrey had seen the big furry creature when Grandpa had slid into the ditch. "What do we do now?" Denny asked, staring into the woods.

"We'll head into the woods in the direction Audrey saw the creature and see if we can find some tracks or something."

Randy gunned the snowmobile motor and drove slowly into the woods. There was no path, so he had to maneuver the machine around trees and look out for bushes and fallen tree trunks and branches. It was slow going.

After a while, Denny took over driving the snowmobile, so Randy could walk ahead and look for tracks. They wove slowly through the woods, looking for clues. It seemed to take forever. The boys would stop occasionally and examine a broken branch or some hair caught on a tree limb. They were becoming discouraged.

"Let's head home," Denny suggested.

"Just a little farther," Randy begged. "I know we'll find something. We just have to be patient."

Denny sighed. "Okay, but I'm getting cold, and it's starting to snow."

The boys continued to weave through the trees.

"Stop!" Randy put up his right hand. "I see some tracks going toward that clearing up ahead. Maybe there is a cabin or something there."

Denny stopped the snowmobile.

"These are really big tracks—like a moose foot," Randy said. He got down on his knees to examine the tracks more closely.

Randy put his foot next to the tracks. "These tracks are twice as big as my foot—and that's pretty big," Randy explained with a loud laugh. "This must be a big person. The tracks don't look exactly human—but then, they aren't animal either."

"Maybe somebody saw us coming and decided to scare us with some fake footprints," Denny suggested with a shiver, "like those big clown feet you can put on when you want to act funny."

Randy shrugged. "Maybe," he said, "and maybe not. I'll follow the footprints, and you can follow me with the snowmobile."

The boys moved slowly, cautiously, through the woods, until they were in the clearing. A small stream, which was frozen over, ran through the center of the clearing, and there were very few large trees in a space about the size of a couple city blocks. It looked as if someone had cleared the trees and stumps out for some reason. The snow was about a foot deep, so it was impossible to see what the ground under the snow looked like.

"This would be a great place to build a cabin," Denny speculated. "Nobody would ever find you out here."

"Yeah," Randy agreed. "But why would you want to live out here in no-man's-land all by yourself?"

Denny shrugged. He didn't know what the answer to that question was.

A light bulb went on in Randy's head. "Unless you don't want anyone to find you!"

"Yeah," Denny agreed. "Maybe a crook would build out here so no one could ever find him and see what he was doing."

The boys stood silently in the center of the clearing, pondering their situation. Only the roar of the snowmobile motor could be heard in the forest. Just then, the snowmobile motor started sputtering and suddenly stopped. Everything became eerily quiet.

Chapter 6

Christmas Preparations

"Don't lick off the frosting knife!" Audrey scolded Ty.

"I thought we were done," Ty answered, licking off his fingers.

"Well, we're not," Hannah said, cutting into the conversation. "Here's another pan of sugar cookies to decorate."

The children had been decorating all kinds of Christmas-shaped cookies with red, green, yellow, blue, and white frosting for about an hour. Hannah had baked the sugar cookies that morning and let them cool.

"I like decorating the Christmas bells," Missy said.

"My favorites are the Santa Clauses," Audrey chimed in.

"I like the Christmas trees," Jenny confessed.

"I think I'll rest," Ty said with a sigh. "I'll take Laddie outside for a potty break."

"Good idea," Jenny said. *He is a poor decorator anyway,* she thought. *Good riddance.*

"Why do you make so many cookies?" Missy asked Hannah.

"I give some of these away as Christmas gifts," Hannah replied. "Some of the older folks in the neighborhood don't bake anymore, so I give cookies for Christmas gifts—they really enjoy them."

"When will you be giving these cookies away?" Missy asked.

"Tomorrow. I'll start in town and then finish at old man Moses's place."

"Who's old man Moses?" Missy asked.

"He's an old guy that lives in the wood, about two miles from here as the crow flies. His full name is Jebediah Moses. He's kind of grumpy—but pretty nice when you get to know him. He lives so deep in the woods that there are no good roads to his place, so I ski over there. I'll do that tomorrow afternoon."

"Can I go along?" Audrey asked with enthusiasm.

"Sure. Can you cross-country ski?"

"No, but I can learn."

"I'll bet you'll catch on quickly," Hannah said, and she smiled. "Anyone else want to come along?"

"Not this time," Jenny replied. "Maybe sometime when you're not going so far—like half a mile."

Missy grinned shyly and shook her head, no.

"Okay," said Hannah. "Then Audrey and I will go alone—unless you want to come along, Abby?" Hannah looked at Abby for an answer.

"Heavens no!" Grandma laughed. "It's been years since I've skied. I'd be so sore after three miles you'd have to carry me home. The next day I wouldn't be able to get out of bed."

Everyone laughed.

* * *

After the girls had finished decorating the cookies, they asked to be excused so they could go to their room to wrap Christmas gifts.

"Do you have wrapping paper and such?" Hannah asked.

"I brought some along," Grandma said. "I'll get them what they need."

Loaded down with brightly colored Christmas paper, Scotch tape, scissors, and name tags, the girls headed to their room in the hunters' lodge.

"Let's get a puppy to play with while we wrap," Jenny suggested.

"Hannah might not like that," Audrey said, shaking her head.

"She won't know—we'll only keep it for an hour and take it back. Come on, Missy. You go with me. We'll sneak out the back way so nobody sees us," Jenny said, grabbing Missy's arm.

The two girls ran across the backyard to the dog barn with no coats or boots on. They entered the barn, where it was cozy and warm, and went to Babe's pen.

"You pet Babe and talk to her, and I'll grab a puppy," Jenny said to Missy.

"What if she gets mad and bites me?"

"She won't—she's really tame. I've been in her pen before."

Missy put her arms around Babe and gave her a hug. She scratched behind Babe's ears and talked to the female husky in a low, calm tone of voice. Babe seemed content and happy to be getting so much attention from Missy.

Jenny sat down in the straw and played with all the puppies for a minute; then she picked up a cream-and-brown-colored puppy, stuck it under her sweatshirt, and left the pen. When she was by the barn door, she called, "Come on, Missy. Babe will never miss one of her puppies."

Missy said goodbye to Babe and the remaining puppies and left the pen, closing the gate behind her.

* * *

Audrey smiled when she saw the puppy under Jenny's sweatshirt. "You're crazy, but that puppy sure is cute."

"We'll take her back in an hour. Now we've got to name her," Jenny said.

"How about Peanut?" Missy suggested. "She's the same colors as a peanut."

"Yes, she is," Audrey agreed.

"Good name, Missy," Jenny said. "Peanut it is." She sat Peanut down on the rug and went to get her presents from her suitcase.

Since the girls had presents for each other and didn't want anyone to see what they were giving, they each went to a different corner of the room with their wrapping supplies. Peanut walked about and explored the room.

"I'm done," Jenny announced a short time later. She wasn't too careful with her wrapping techniques.

"So am I," Missy said.

"Wait just a minute more, and I'll be done," Audrey promised.

"We'll take Peanut out into the hall and play with her until you're done. Call us in when you're ready," Missy suggested.

"Okay."

As Missy crossed the room to pick up Peanut, she stepped into something wet. "Oh no," she wailed. "I think Peanut did a naughty-naughty."

"Take off your sock and put it into the bathroom sink," Jenny suggested. "We can wash it out later."

Missy put the wet sock into the sink and washed off her foot while Jenny held Peanut. Then the girls took the puppy into the hall to play.

Peanut loved to crawl over anyone on the floor and chase the girls when they scurried across the floor on hands and knees.

Audrey soon joined in the fun. Peanut yipped happily as she chased the girls, nipping at their heels and rolling on the floor like a big fur ball when she tried to jump into the air to catch a ball they tossed.

"Time to take her back before Grandma and Hannah call us to help with supper," Audrey said.

"Will do," Jenny said as she and Missy headed out the back door of the lodge with the tired puppy hidden safely under Jenny's sweatshirt.

"I wonder what those girls are running to the dog barn for?" Hannah asked while peering out the kitchen window. "They haven't got on coats or boots."

"They're probably returning the puppy they took from the barn an hour ago," Grandma said with a knowing smile. "I was looking out the window about an hour ago when I saw them coming from the barn. Jenny had a big, wiggly lump under her sweatshirt."

Hannah let out a loud burst of laughter. *Kids will be kids,* she thought, remembering when she had been young and loved to sneak pets into the house.

*   *   *

Basil chopping wood

Basil finished splitting logs for the day around three o'clock. Then he loaded Josh and himself up with firewood for the stove. As the two adults headed to the house, they saw Ty outside, playing with Laddie. "Want to come with us to cut down a Christmas tree?" Basil asked Ty.

"Sure!" Ty said excitedly. "Where do we look?"

Basil chuckled. "The whole woods around this place are full of pine trees. I guess we can look anywhere."

"I'll get the ax," Josh volunteered.

"We'll wait here by the kitchen shed," Basil said.

A few minute later, Josh showed up with a sharp ax. The two men and Ty headed into the woods in back of the hunting lodge.

"I saw some young trees out this way last summer," Basil said. "I'm sure we can find one that will suit Hannah—she's awful fussy," he added with a wink of his eye directed at Ty.

"I get you." Josh laughed. "I've got a wife like that too."

They trudged through the deep snow for a few blocks and then stopped in an area where a dozen young trees were growing.

"Which one do you like, Ty?" Basil asked.

"That one." Ty pointed to the largest tree in the area.

"That's too big." Basil shook his head, no.

"How about that one?" Ty pointed to a tree that Laddie was sniffing around.

"Looks good," Basil said as he walked over to the tree and began clearing the snow around the bottom of the tree trunk.

Laddie barked louder, and a squirrel jumped out on top of Basil.

Ty fell backward with a scream.

Josh burst out laughing, as the frightened squirrel scampered across the snow as fast as his legs could carry him, with Laddie in hot pursuit.

"Laddie saved us from being attacked by that squirrel," Ty said excitedly.

The men laughed loudly.

"Yup, that was a killer squirrel," Josh said with a straight face.

"Good thing Laddie scared that squirrel out of that tree before I hit it with my ax," Basil joked. "It might have clawed me to death."

It only took a few swipes of the ax, and the tree fell over. Josh grabbed hold of the trunk and Basil took hold of the top of the tree. They picked it up and headed back to the inn. It was beginning to snow and get colder.

"You can carry the ax, Ty," Basil said, handing the ax to the boy. "Laddie can look out for killer squirrels that might attack us for cutting down their trees."

Everyone laughed. Even Ty began to see the humor in what had just happened.

*   *   *

"I'm worried about the boys," Grandma told Grandpa when they brought the tree into the great room to set it up. "It's started to snow and blow, and they aren't home yet."

"We'll wait a little longer—then we'll go look for them. Do you girls have any idea where they went?" Grandpa asked Audrey.

"W-well," Audrey stammered. She didn't want to tell Grandpa that the boys were hunting for clues to solve the Bigfoot mystery.

"Well what?" Grandpa gave Audrey a stern look. "You'd better tell us what you know. If the boys get caught out in this snowstorm, they could die."

"All I know is they went back on the road where we slid into the ditch. They were planning to go into the woods where I saw the big furry creature and look for him."

"Oh, those silly kids," Grandma scolded. "There are no big hairy creatures around here. I just hope they didn't get lost."

"Or that the snowmobile didn't quit on them," Basil added.

"The storm is picking up fast," Grandpa said, with a worried look on his face. "It will be dark soon. If they don't come back before dark, it will really be hard to find them."

"I agree with Josh," Basil said.

The men put on many layers of warm clothing and their face masks. They were preparing for the cold wind and snow.

"I'm coming too," Hannah announced as she put on her warm winter parka. I know this forest better than anyone else. Maybe I can be of some help."

"Okay. Let's take my old four-wheel-drive pickup," Basil suggested. "It won't get stuck as easily as your van."

As the three adults drove off into the snowstorm, Grandma Abby folded her hands and said a prayer. She knew, from her own experiences living through many cold winters, that being caught in a snowstorm was not a fun thing.

Chapter 7

Lost in a Snowstorm

"Now what?" Denny looked at Randy, and there was fear in his eyes.

"Let's try to start it," Randy suggested. "We have to make sure we don't flood the motor."

The boys tried in vain to start the snowmobile. After several minutes of failure, the machine went dead. The boys knew it was hopeless.

"We can't push it all the way back to the lodge, so we'll have to leave it here," Denny said sadly.

"It's starting to snow and get colder," Randy said. "We'd better get going. We're about half an hour from home on foot. We can still see the snowmobile tracks. If the wind comes up and covers the tracks, we're in big trouble."

It was hard walking in the deep snow. The boys walked for about fifteen minutes, while the wind became stronger and colder. The snow began to fall and blow in large white sheets. Soon it was impossible to see more than twenty feet ahead. The snowmobile tracks were now drifted over.

"I'm cold and tired," Denny complained.

"We can't stop now, buddy," Randy ordered. "If we do, we'll freeze to death."

"Whose dumb idea was this, anyway?" Denny whined.

"Doesn't matter," Randy answered calmly. "We've got to figure out something. I've heard that sometimes people bury themselves in the snow until the storm is over. It's warmer in the snow than out here in the wind."

The boys sat down in the deep snow, next to a large tree so they would have some protection from the wind. They huddled together and pulled their coat hoods over their faces. They sat silently, wondering what to do next.

*   *   *

"Did you see that?" Randy whispered to Denny.

"What?" Denny asked. He had his ears covered with his cap and coat hood and couldn't hear very well.

"Shhhh! Not so loud. I think I saw something moving in the trees over there."

The boys sat frozen in terror. Out of the storm appeared a big black wolf. Denny gasped and clung to Randy.

"It's okay," Randy whispered. "I know how to handle wolves. My Uncle Lone Wolf told me how. Let me go, and I'll show you."

Denny dug his fingers into Randy's coat and hung on for dear life.

"It's okay, honest," Randy said softly. "We Indians think wolves are very clever and consider them brothers. If this guy is the leader of his pack, all we have to do is show him respect and he'll leave us alone."

Denny didn't let go. "I can't—I'm scared," he stammered.

"Don't show fear. Stay calm—then he'll treat you as an equal," Randy assured Denny.

Denny didn't let go.

Big black wolf snarling

Randy pried Denny's fingers off his jacket and began crawling toward the large black wolf. *Stare him down. Don't show fear,* Randy repeated to himself as he crawled toward the wolf, whose lips were pulled back, with his teeth showing, as a low growl came from his throat.

Randy crawled slowly toward the large wolf, pausing at times and lying quietly, patiently, waiting for some signal from the wolf that might show he was friendly. The wolf's teeth were still showing, but his tail began wagging slightly.

Slowly, slowly, Randy crawled over to where the black wolf was standing and tried to make friends with him.

Randy rolled over on his back in front of the large male wolf to pay homage to the animal. The wolf looked down at Randy with his yellow jewel-like eyes. Randy lifted his head under the wolf's throat and gently bit his chin. The wolf didn't move. Randy was acknowledging the wolf as the leader and showing the wolf that he didn't want to challenge him.

Then Randy reached into his coat pocket and pulled out his gingerbread-man cookie that Hannah had given him in case he got hungry. He offered the cookie to the wolf. The wolf took the cookie and sat down on all four feet to eat it.

Be calm—be patient—don't move, Randy repeated to himself.

After what seemed like a long time, the wolf got up, sniffed Randy, sprayed him with a fluid from the top of his tail and walked toward the woods.

Randy breathed a sigh of relief, and Denny nearly passed out.

The wolf stopped, looked back at the boys, walked forward a few more steps, and stopped again. Then he turned and started walking toward Randy. Then he stopped, turned, and started walking toward the woods again.

"I think he wants us to follow him," Randy said softly to Denny. "Come on."

Denny hesitated. He just wanted the wolf to leave.

"Come on—it's okay. He knows the way to the lodge—I'll bet on that."

Randy got up and followed the wolf into the woods. Denny stood up and ran after Randy.

The wolf picked up the pace, and soon the boys were running along a well-traveled path through the woods. The path had been packed down by wolves traveling through the area the past few days. The new snow was blowing on the path, but the snow underneath was hard.

After about five minutes, Denny sat down on the path, exhausted. "I just have to rest," he said breathlessly.

Randy stopped to see what was the matter with Denny. The wolf disappeared into the forest.

"Shoot!" Randy shook his head in disgust. "I think we've lost the wolf."

Denny sat in the path with his head hanging down, trying to catch his breath.

After a few minutes, Randy helped Denny stand up, and they started walking in the direction where the wolf had disappeared. Sure enough, there was the wolf, lying in the path, waiting for the boys.

The wolf took off running again, and the boys ran after him in hot pursuit. This process was repeated three times, and then the wolf stopped suddenly next to a dark object that loomed before them.

The boys walked closer to the wolf. "It's the dog barn!" Denny shouted hysterically. "It's the dog barn! He brought us home!" Denny reached into his pocket and pulled out his gingerbread-man cookie. "Here." He handed the cookie to the wolf, who grabbed it and ran off into the forest.

Randy laughed. "That big black wolf knew where he was going all the time. I'll bet that wolf was Chico, the father of Delilah's puppies. He knows where his wife and family live. He probably hangs out around here all the time."

*   *   *

Grandma Abby heard something in the back shed. She thought the men and Hannah had returned. When she saw the two boys come through the kitchen door, she put both hands over her heart and stopped breathing.

"Thank God!" she gasped. "Where have you two been? We've been frantically trying to find you."

"We're okay," Randy assured her, "but do we have a story to tell."

"Yeah," Denny grinned. "When everyone gets here, we'll tell you all a really wild story—you won't believe this."

Grandma was too happy to scold the boys. She whispered a prayer of thanks and gave each boy a big hug and kiss on the cheek. Then she got on her cell phone and called Basil, Josh, and Hannah to tell them the boys were home.

The boys blushed in embarrassment when Grandma kissed them; however, they preferred being kissed to being scolded, so they didn't say a word as they went into the great room and tried to thaw themselves in front of the big open fireplace that was roaring with a blazing fire of red-hot logs.

*   *   *

At the supper table the boys told their story. The girls listened, wide-eyed and fascinated. Ty's eyes were big as saucers, and his mouth hung open. He was visualizing the wolf eating the two boys, as the wolf in *The Gingerbread Man* fairy tale had eaten the gingerbread man, in one gulp.

"Wow," Jenny said with admiration in her voice when the story was completed. "You were sure brave, Randy. I would have wet my pants."

Everyone laughed.

"Brave, but foolish," Grandpa Josh commented.

"It was nothing," Randy said modestly. "I knew all about wolves from my Uncle Lone Wolf."

Audrey sighed. "You're lucky Lone Wolf knew what he was talking about, or you'd both be frozen solid by now," she said.

"Oh, let's not talk about it," Hannah suggested. "Let's just be thankful it all worked out okay."

"I think Hannah was the real hero." Randy grinned. "When I handed Chico that gingerbread-man cookie, and he ate it, I knew I had a friend for life!"

Chapter 8

Christmas Carols

Having ten people decorate a Christmas tree turned out to be a real challenge. While Hannah divided the decorations among the six children, so each one could put some on the tree, Grandpa and Basil put up the colorful lights and then sat down to admire their work.

The children gathered around the tree to decorate. Ty put his ornaments at the very bottom of the tree, because he was the shortest. Missy, Jenny, and Denny put their decorations above Ty's, and Audrey and Randy put theirs as high up as they could reach.

Missy and Jenny had strung a line of popcorn earlier that day, so they put the long line of puffy white popcorn around the middle of the tree.

"That looks silly when there is only popcorn around the middle of the tree," Audrey commented.

"Sorry," Hannah said. "That's all the popcorn I had available today. I'll make some more tomorrow, and we'll put it around the top and bottom of the tree."

Fireplace and Christmas tree

The big argument started when it was time to put the beautiful silver star at the very top of the three. All of the children wanted to do that.

"We'll have to pick numbers," Grandma suggested when the arguing escalated.

Basil went to get the ladder, while each child picked a number between one and twenty. Missy was the closest, with number sixteen. The right number was seventeen.

Missy climbed up the ladder very carefully, holding the beautiful star. She placed it on the very top of the tree and asked, "Does that look straight?"

"Yes," Hannah answered," it looks fine to me."

Grandma gave her opinion. "Me too."

Basil turned on the lights, and everyone clapped and cheered. They all agreed the tree looked beautiful.

"Go over and look out the big window," Basil suggested. "We've put up some more lights outside."

The group gathered around the picture window in the great room, while Basil went to the garage to turn on the lights.

"Oh! Wow! Great!" were comments heard as the multicolored lights shone on the shrubs in front of the window as well as on the two evergreen trees growing in the front yard.

"Good job," Grandma complimented Basil when he came back to the great room. "Now we'll have to sing some Christmas Carols to celebrate the start of the Christmas festivities."

Grandma Abby sat down by the old upright piano next to the fireplace and began playing "Deck the Halls," an old Welsh carol. Basil grabbed his guitar and joined in.

"Grab those carol books on the coffee table," Grandma instructed as she joyfully banged away on the piano.

The children and Grandpa did as they were told and joined in the singing. Grandma sang soprano, Hannah sang alto, Grandpa sang tenor, and Basil sang bass. The children sang the melody, each in his or her own way. It was a joyful, lovely sound.

Next the group sang "Angels We Have Heard on High," a French carol, which was followed by "Away in a Manger," a German carol. Then Grandma played "O Come All Ye Faithful," a Latin hymn.

"We can end this international song fest with 'We Wish You a Merry Christmas,' an English carol," Grandma said.

"Oh no, you don't," Hannah protested. "We can't quit until we sing a popular and simple Norwegian carol called '*Jeg Er Sa Glad.*'"

"What does that mean?" Ty asked, wrinkling his nose.

"*Jeg Er Sa Glad* is Norwegian for 'I Am So Glad' in English," Hannah replied. "Come now, and I'll teach you a few verses. There are seven of them—too much to learn at one time!" Hannah said with a laugh.

Hannah began singing in her beautiful alto voice, while Basil accompanied her on his guitar: "I am so glad each Christmas Eve, the night of Jesus's birth. Then, like the sun, the star shone forth, and angels sang on earth."

"Now, all of you try it," Hannah said, encouraging the group to join her.

After teaching the first verse, Hannah sang the second verse. "The little child of Bethlehem, he was a king indeed; for he came down from heaven above, to help a world in need."

Everyone sang the second verse.

"Great!" Hannah exclaimed. "Now we'll do the last verse: "And so I love each Christmas Eve, and I love Jesus too; and that he loves me every day, I know so well is true."

"Very good!" Hannah clapped as she blew kisses to the children.

"One more verse of 'We Wish You a Merry Christmas,' and then you are all excused," Grandma said as she started playing the song on the piano.

"It's getting late," Grandpa announced after the sounds from the piano and guitar had ceased. He got out of his chair and started up the stairs. Grandpa was tired from all the activity that day. *I guess I'm not as young as I used to be,* he muttered to himself. *I wish I had the energy that those children have,* he thought as he slowly climbed the stairs to his bedroom.

Chapter 9

A Grinch on the Loose?

"They're gone!' Ty shouted, bursting into the kitchen, where the rest of the family was having breakfast.

"Stay right there, young man!" Grandma ordered. "Take off your boots in the shed. They are covered with snow."

"What's gone?" Hannah asked in a calm voice while flipping pancakes on her old cooking range.

Ty sat down on the kitchen floor and took off his snow boots. "The Christmas-tree lights from outside. I saw tracks too—leading into the woods—when I took Laddie out to potty this morning."

Everyone started talking at once about the lights and what could have happened to them.

"Sit down and have some breakfast before everything gets cold," Grandma ordered over the noisy talk around the table.

Ty pulled a chair up to the big round oak table and filled his plate with pancakes. "Pass the syrup, please," he said to Audrey, who had the syrup sitting in front of her.

The noise grew louder as everyone expressed an opinion on the mystery of the missing lights.

Grandpa lost his patience with all the loud talking around the table. "Quiet!" he ordered. "Let's talk one at a time, as civilized people do."

"Well," Audrey spoke boldly, "I believe that big furry creature I saw in the woods took them. He's like the Grinch—in the children's book—who stole Christmas."

"There are no hairy monsters in the woods!" Randy declared emphatically. "It's some mean neighbor who doesn't like Christmas."

"I think it's Chico," Denny speculated. "He knows how to bring us home, so he might also know how to steal lights."

"What kind of footprints did you see outside?" Basil asked Ty.

"I don't know," Ty muttered, with his mouth full of food.

"Let the boy eat!" Hannah gave Basil a stern look. "You can get dressed and go outside after breakfast and check the footprints out for yourself."

"Yes," Grandpa agreed with Hannah. "All of you get dressed and go outside, so it gets quiet in here."

"You sure are grouchy today," Grandma commented, taking a good look at Grandpa. "Are you feeling all right?"

"I'm fine," Grandpa insisted. "I just want less noise. My hearing aid is going crazy trying to adjust to all this noise. I think that I'll go out to the barns and feed the dogs. They are quiet when they eat."

Grandpa excused himself from the table and went out into the shed to get dressed for outdoors.

One by one the family members got up from the table and gathered their outdoor clothing from the shed. They brought things into the kitchen to get warmed up.

"I can't find my gloves,' Denny whined.

"Where did you take them off?" Grandma asked.

"In the shed, and I put them in my coat pocket."

"Then go look in the shed. They may have fallen out of your coat pocket."

"Someone took my scarf!" Jenny complained.

"Since three of you have identical scarves, you'd better all check the shed for your scarves," Hannah suggested. "There are also extra scarves and mittens in that box in the corner by the cooking range. Check it out."

"Whew!" Hannah declared when all the children were finally dressed and gone. "Help me make ten boxes of cookies, Abby, and then you and I will deliver them to the old folks in town."

"Thanks." Grandma gave a sigh of relief. "I'll be happy to get away from here for a couple hours. A little peace and quiet would be welcome."

* * *

"Those tracks don't look human," Basil speculated. "They look more like a big bear's tracks."

"Are there any bears in the woods?" Denny asked.

"Yes, but I don't know any that steal Christmas lights," Basil said with a chuckle.

"I still think it's someone dressed like a bear, trying to scare us," Randy said.

"Why would anyone try to scare us?" Basil asked.

"That's the mystery," Randy replied. "If we knew the answer to that question, we could solve the mystery."

"Isn't Bigfoot half human and half beast?" Audrey asked.

"I don't know," Basil replied. "I've never seen him."

"Maybe it's a her," Jenny suggested.

"Maybe," Basil agreed. "Let's follow these tracks and see if we can find the tree lights. We're lucky the snowing and blizzard stopped in the middle of the night, or there wouldn't be any track to follow. Whoever took the lights did it early this morning, before we were all up."

Audrey and Basil by Lake Toby

"It looks like the crook dropped some lights here and dragged them for some distance," Basil said after the group had followed the footprints along the shore of the lake for about half a mile.

"He or she crossed the lake here," Basil said, pointing. "It went into the woods over there. We know what direction it's heading. We'll take up the chase again later. We've got work to do at home. We'd better get back."

"Ohhh," the children moaned. They all wanted to continue the pursuit, but Basil didn't seem that interested in spending his morning trying to find some old tree lights.

"Can't we go on?" Audrey asked politely. "We'll do our chores later."

"Well, maybe a few of you can go," Basil said. "We'll let the girls go today, because the boys were out yesterday. Remember to mark your path and be home for lunch—no later!" Basil warned.

"Come on, you two," Basil said to Randy and Denny. "Let's feed dogs, shovel snow, and chop wood. That should keep you from getting lost today."

Randy and Denny followed Basil back to the dog barn without a word of complaint. They were happy they hadn't been grounded for their bad decision the day before.

*　*　*

The girls had followed the track for about half a mile. "Look over there—something red is sticking out of the snow," Missy shouted and pointed with glee. They had been marking their way with an occasional tree branch. That had been Missy's idea. She'd thought it would be better than using bread crumbs, as Hansel and Gretel had done in the fairy tale.

The girls ran to the spot, about twenty yards off the ski trail, where the red specks showed up in the snow.

Sure enough, half buried in the new-fallen snow, were two long strands of red Christmas lights. While Jenny and Missy dug the lights out of the snow and wound them into a circle so they could carry them home, Audrey looked around the area.

"I found some animal tracks over here too," Audrey said. "They look like a big dog's tracks or maybe a wolf. The tracks seem to have come out of the woods suddenly, followed the Bigfoot tracks for a distance, and then disappeared back into the woods."

"Let's get out of here," Jenny suggested, wide-eyed. "I don't want to deal with any wolf."

"Me either," Missy agreed.

"Maybe the wolf chased Bigfoot, until he dropped the lights so he could run faster and get away from the wolf," Audrey reasoned, trying to make sense of the footprints going in different directions after they had gone in the same direction for a short distance.

"Maybe—who cares?" Jenny said sarcastically. "We've got the lights, so let's head for home. We're at least a mile from home, and we don't want to get caught in a snowstorm, like the dumb boys did."

"For once I agree with you," Audrey said and smiled. "Besides, all the tracks lead into the dense forest over there, and we could get lost if we get off this ski path."

The girls chatted nervously as they hurried home. They kept looking over their shoulders to make sure they weren't being chased by any wolf. They were happy they had found the lights. They were also getting very cold.

*   *   *

At lunch, Grandma and Hannah talked about all the old folks they had given cookies to and how much the elders had appreciated the gifts.

Basil, Randy, and Denny bragged about all the wood they had chopped and hauled into the shed.

Grandpa and Ty told stories about feeding the dogs and playing with the puppies. Grandpa too had enjoyed playing with the puppies. It had reminded him of his youth and the farm he'd been raised on in South Dakota, where they'd always had puppies.

The three girls had the best story to tell, about finding the lights and their theory of how a wolf had chased Bigfoot until he dropped the lights in the snow.

"Whatever chased that crook must have frightened him enough to drop the lights." Hannah agreed that far with the girls' theory.

"Maybe the monster dropped the lights because he didn't really want them—he just didn't want us to use them. Maybe he's just mean and wants to steal Christmas, like the Grinch did," Ty said after listening to the girls' story.

Basil chuckled. "Maybe we do have a Grinch out there in the woods trying to steal our Christmas," he speculated, "but we're not going to let him do that—are we?"

"No!" all the children shouted at once.

Chapter 10

Skiing is Hard!

"Cross-country skis are different than downhill skis," Hannah instructed Audrey as she handed her a set of skis. The two were going to visit Jebediah Moses, who lived about three miles into the dense woods.

"These skis are shorter and narrower, so your weight is distributed more evenly, which will allow you to move more quickly. The tips of the skis are higher and more curved to better cut through the deep snow."

Audrey put her skis on the floor, stood on the ski binding with her special ski boots, clipped the toes of the boots to the bindings while the heel remained free, and stood up straight. "Now what?" she asked.

"Let's start without poles," Hannah suggested. "Move your right arm and opposite leg forward at the same time—gliding along." Hannah demonstrated. "Glide as long as you can on each ski. The top part of your body can lean forward."

Audrey tried Hannah's instructions. "I'm moving," she shouted with glee.

Audrey getting ready to ski

"Good job," Hannah said with a grin. "Take a few quick steps and then glide on a ski as long as possible. Keep your arms swinging by your sides, parallel to the track. Your arms should extend in front and in back of you—opposite arm with leg."

After Audrey had practiced for a few minutes, Hannah handed her a set of poles. "These poles are used for steadiness and propulsion," Hannah said. "They are made of aluminum, so they are lightweight. The spikes at the end provide fixed pivots when the poles go through the snow crest. The disks above the spikes will keep the poles from going into the snow too far. Poles give you extra push. I think this size of pole will be right for you, Audrey. If they are too long, let me know."

Audrey fastened the poles to her wrists with the straps attached to the poles, so she wouldn't drop them. Then she practiced for a few yards.

"I'm ready," she announced.

"Okay, let's go." Hannah picked up her backpack with the cookies inside and started down the ski trail. "I'll lead and cut a track for you. Follow in my track, and it will be much easier," she instructed Audrey.

"Stride, reach, glide," Audrey repeated to herself while trying to maintain a steady rhythm. She swooshed through the powdery snow while the cold wind bit at her face. Her sunglasses helped protect her eyes, but the cold penetrated her forehead, cheeks, and chin. Audrey stopped and pulled her warm cap down to her eyes and wrapped her long scarf around her chin and cheeks. Only her mouth and eyes were visible.

The rhythm of her arms and legs working in tandem deepened her heartbeat as the cold air filled her lungs. After a short period of time, she shouted ahead to Hannah, "I've got to rest—this is hard!"

Hannah stopped and sat down in the snow. "We'll rest a few minutes. You're going great. We'll go a little slower for a while."

The two skiers made steady progress, even if they did rest every ten minutes. They skied deeper and deeper into the woods, following a trail made by the animals that lived there.

"About half a mile to go," Hannah announced at their fourth rest stop.

"I hope I can make it. My legs and arms are screaming to stop," Audrey whined.

"If you feel you can't go anymore, we'll stop and carry our skis for a while. Walking will relax your muscles a bit," Hannah informed Audrey, who was lying in the snow like a dead person.

As the skiers entered a clearing in the woods, they could see a small cabin in the distance. "There it is!" Audrey shouted excitedly.

"Yes, and there's smoke coming out of the chimney, so it will be warm inside. We'll ask Jeb if we can sit awhile," Hannah said.

The skiers took off their skis on the porch and knocked at the door. It took a few minutes for the old man to come to the door.

"I wonder why it's taking so long?" Audrey questioned.

"He's probably tidying up. It's pretty messy in there. Womenfolk scare old Moses." Hannah chuckled.

Finally, after what seemed like a lifetime, the old man opened the door.

"Hello, Miss Hannah," he said with a slight smile. "I was kind of expecting you. You usually pay a visit this time of year."

"Hello, Jeb. It's nice to see you again." Hannah put out her hand, and Jeb shook it. "This is my cousin Abby's Granddaughter, Audrey. She wanted to ski along with me to see where you lived."

Jeb said, "Hello, Audrey," but never invited the women to come inside.

He was a short, stooped man with white hair. His weathered face, partially hidden by a large handlebar mustache, looked tired and lonely.

"I brought you some Christmas cookies," Hannah said as she opened her backpack. She handed Jeb the cookie tin.

He took the tin and said, "Thank you," but didn't move away from the door. It was almost as if he didn't want the women to come inside his cabin.

"Could we come inside to warm up and rest a bit?" Hannah asked.

Jeb didn't answer.

"Please," Audrey begged. "I'm very cold and tired. It's my first time out skiing."

Jeb looked at Audrey's slumped body, and his heart melted.

"Well, I suppose—for a while—I need to go someplace soon," Jeb said in a grumpy tone of voice.

The women entered the cabin and sat down by the fireplace. It was toasty-warm and cozy. Audrey noticed some fancy cowboy boots by the fireplace and two empty coffee cups on the sturdy homemade table in the middle of the room. There seemed to be two small doors leading off the main room of the cabin. *It looks like someone else lives here with Jeb,* she thought.

"How have you been?" Hannah asked. "I think of you often and hope you are okay."

"That's kind of you, Miss Hannah. I'm fine—a little arthritis now and then."

Hannah laughed. "I know what you mean," she said.

Old man Moses did manage a slight smile, but his eyes kept darting around the room as if he were nervous.

The conversation continued about the weather, holiday season, and clearing of the trees from the woods. Hannah did most of the talking, while Jeb listened and shook his head in agreement some of the time.

"You sure have cleared a lot of trees in this area lately. Are you planning to plant some crop or something?" Hannah asked.

"No, just need firewood," Jeb answered in a casual tone of voice.

Audrey sat by the fire and looked all around the room, trying to memorize every item. She had a weird feeling that something was wrong, but she didn't quite know what it was.

Finally Hannah stood up. "We'd better head back. It will take a while longer to get back, because Audrey is already pooped out. We want to get home before dark."

"Nice of you to come, Miss Hannah and Miss Audrey," Jeb said quietly.

"You take care of yourself, and if you need anything at all, let Basil or me know—okay?"

"I will, and thanks for the cookies," Jeb said as the women headed for the door. He closed the door immediately after they left.

The women took their skis off the porch and put them in the snow, snapped their boots onto the skis, and headed home using the same track they had come on.

It took longer to get home because they walked the last mile. Audrey decided she just couldn't ski another inch.

It was nice to see the smoke curling from the Husky Hideaway chimney as they came out of the woods and crossed Lake Toby.

"Home sweet home," Audrey mumbled to herself as they crossed the lake. *How good it will feel to rest on my bed for a while before supper,* she thought.

* * *

The supper table was lively with conversation about the day's events. Since it was Christmas Eve, the family had planned to go to the candlelight service at the small country church nearby. The service wasn't until eight o'clock, so they had plenty of time to visit.

Audrey didn't want to tell the adults about what she had seen in Jeb's cabin. She had planned to wait until the next Peanut Butter Club meeting to talk about her observations. However, Hannah did bring up the subject.

"Jeb sure was acting strange today. He's not the friendliest person in the world, but today he was really cool," she said.

"Did he seem sick or something?" Basil asked.

"I asked him how he felt, and he said, 'fine,'" Hannah answered.

"Oh well." Basil shook his head. "He's getting old, so maybe he just didn't want to talk."

"I'm not so sure someone that old should live alone in the woods," Hannah said. "Maybe his nephew will come and stay with him. Mason sometimes comes for a visit. I'm not sure what Mason is doing now. Maybe he's got a job and can't come to stay."

"That would be the day—when Mason gets a job," Basil said with disgust. "I've never seen such a worthless person. He's in his late twenties and can't seem to hold a steady job—never has, as far as I know."

"Well, it's Christmas Eve, so let's talk about something besides Mason," Hannah suggested.

"Good idea," Audrey said, wanting to change the conversation. "Will we be opening our Christmas presents tonight after the church service?"

"We always open our presents on Christmas Eve," Jenny said.

"Sounds like a plan," Basil said and chuckled. "That way we'll have more time to do other things on Christmas day. And," he added, "I won't be able to sleep thinking about all the presents I'm getting." He winked at Ty.

Ty grinned. He was thinking the same thing.

Chapter 11

Christmas Eve

The candlelight service at the church was lovely, but Ty couldn't wait to get back to the Husky Hideaway. When the candles were finally blown out and the closing hymn, "Joy to the World," had been sung, Ty broke for the aisle so he could get out of the church first.

Grandpa Josh grabbed Ty by his coat collar. "What's your hurry, young man?" he asked. "You act like the church is on fire."

"I want to get home and see how Laddie's doing," Ty lied.

"Laddie is fine," Grandpa assured Ty as he took the boy's hand. "We'll wait politely for our turn to leave. We don't want to run people over—do we?"

"No," Ty said meekly as he stood politely by Grandpa's side.

"The service was lovely," Grandma Abby said to Hannah as they exited the front door of the small church.

"Yes, it was," Hannah agreed. "We'd better get home and set out the Christmas goodies before Santa comes. He might want to have a snack with us." Hannah smiled and winked at Missy, who was walking beside her.

*   *   *

"Santa was here!" Ty shouted as he entered the great room at the inn. "Look at all the presents he brought!"

The children all rushed to the tree and saw the new presents that had been put there while they were at church.

The children looked through the new packages to make sure they each had a gift. The noise level rose to a loud roar as each discovered his or her own package. Then the shaking and guessing began, while Hannah and Grandma put food out on the dining room table. They set out paper plates and cups so everyone could snack as the group opened their presents. The sandwiches, deviled eggs, Christmas breads, and a variety of Christmas cookies made a lovely display on the beautiful old oak table.

"Can we sort these presents into stacks for each person?" Jenny asked.

"Okay," Basil answered. "You can put all my presents here beside my chair." Basil settled down in his large reclining chair and pulled out his harmonica. He played Christmas carols on the harmonica as the children sorted out gifts and made piles for each person.

The laughter, noise, and good cheer grew louder as the process moved forward. Soon all the gifts were sorted.

"We'll take turns opening gifts," Grandma announced. "That way we can all see what everyone gets. We'll start with Ty, the youngest, and end with Grandpa—he's the oldest."

Ty tore into his biggest package. It was from Santa Claus. Ty had written to Santa a month ago and hoped Santa had gotten his letter.

"Oh boy!" Ty shouted as he opened his box. "Santa got my letter. I wanted a baseball glove and he brought me a beautiful one." Ty hugged his glove and smelled the leather. "Thanks, Santa," he whispered softly into glove.

Missy was next. Her present from Santa was a paint-by-number set. "Thanks, Santa," she said shyly as she held the set up for all to see. Missy loved to paint and was looking forward to painting the picture of a beautiful Indian pony like her own.

Jenny followed Missy. She got a new pair of blue jeans from Santa. "Just what I wanted," she cried, beaming as she ran for the bathroom to put them on.

Denny got a new computer game. "Thanks, Santa," he said with a big grin. Denny loved to play computer games.

Randy got a new ice hockey stick. He was on his junior-high hockey team but didn't have a stick of his own. "Thanks, Santa," he said happily. "Now I can practice at home."

Audrey opened her gift slowly and carefully. She wanted to save the beautiful wrapping and ribbon. The Harry Potter book collection she found inside made her scream with delight. "Now I have my own Harry Potter books, and I can read them as often as I want! Thanks, Santa."

Hannah was the first adult to open a present. "Let's see what Santa brought me," she said with a smile.

Hannah opened her small package carefully and found a jewelry box. Inside was a pewter broach decorated with pearls and a matching set of earrings. "This is beautiful," Hannah gasped. "Thanks, Santa."

Basil's first gift was a new leather billfold. "Now, if I only had some money to put into this," he said jokingly. "Thanks, Santa." Everyone laughed.

Grandma Abby opened her gift and found a designer scarf. "This will match my winter coat perfectly." She was beaming. "Thanks Santa."

Grandpa Josh was last. "It's about time!" he grumbled, while lowering his head so the children couldn't see the smile on his face. "A collection of DVDs with John Wayne movies! The Duke is my favorite cowboy. Thanks, Santa." *I'll enjoy these when I get home in the peace and quiet of my own living room,* he thought as he carefully put the DVDs back into the box.

They continued opening their gifts from family and friends. The excitement grew with each gift. There were board games, books, clothing, knickknacks, card games, and a variety of homemade gifts like jewelry, picture frames, belts, slippers, and candles.

*   *   *

When the last gift had been opened and displayed, Grandma announced, "Now let's clean up all the boxes and wrappings, and then we'll play some games."

Everyone was talking happily as they helped clean up and then gathered up their gifts and took them to their bedrooms. When they returned, Grandma made a suggestion: "Since it's Hannah's house, let's have her choose the first games."

"I choose charades," Hannah said.

"What are charades?" Jenny questioned.

"Charades is an old guessing game played in eighteenth-century France. It's a great party game, because lots of people can play at the same time," Hannah explained. "I'll teach you the rules and some of the strategies—then we'll try it. The females will play against the males."

"We'll whip their butts," Basil said, rubbing his hands together. "I'm pretty good at this."

Hannah ignored his comments and went on to explain. "We'll need a timer, a piece of paper to keep score, a pencil, and two jars. We have to decide how long each team will get to solve the puzzle—anywhere from three to five minutes."

Hannah went to get the supplies from the desk in the living room.

"How about three minutes?" Audrey said.

"Okay," Hannah agreed while handing Audrey the timer and score pad. "You can keep score."

"Since it's Christmas Eve, we'll use a Christmas theme. Each team member will write the name of a movie, book, song, character, or food that is connected to Christmas on a slip of paper and fold that paper and put it into their jar."

There was much talking and confusion until everyone finally had a Christmas-related item written on their slip of paper.

"Good," Hannah said when everyone was done. "Now, when it's your turn, you'll have to pick a piece of paper from the other team's jar and try to act the item out with signals and gestures, so your team can guess what was written on the paper. Remember, you can't speak or make any sounds. You stop when your team guesses the title or the time runs out. We'll record how long it took your team to guess. That will make a difference in the score at the end. The less time it takes, the better your score will be. If you guess the item on the paper, your team will get five points. The teams will take turns. Everyone has to act out one item—then the game will be over. We also count the number of clues it takes to guess each item, so try to give good clues."

"I'm confused," Denny whined.

"I'll demonstrate before we start," Hannah said. "That way you can learn what some of the clues should be."

"If you want to indicate a book title, put your hands together like you were praying and then unfold them slowly." Hannah demonstrated.

"To indicate a movie, form an O with one hand and pantomime cranking with the other hand to show you are operating an old-fashioned movie camera." Hannah again demonstrated.

"To indicate a character, point to yourself. To indicate a song, move your lips like you are singing." Hannah demonstrated singing, and everyone laughed.

"To indicate a food, pretend you are eating." Hannah demonstrated once more. "Okay? Anyone have any questions?" It was silent. "If not, I'll go first for our team, and Basil will go first for his team, because we know how to play. You'll all get the idea as we go along. Let's start."

Hannah and Basil were very good charade players, and before they were done with their turns, everyone had a good idea how to play the game.

Everyone had a great time playing. Even Missy, who was usually very shy about getting up before people and doing anything, did a great job when it was her turn. Everyone cheered her on, and she completed her item in only two minutes.

The females beat the males, but they had all enjoyed the game so much they didn't care who won.

*   *   *

The next game the group played was hearts. Since they had all played this game before, it didn't take too long to explain the rules, which were very simple.

"With ten players, each player gets five cards, and the last two go into the kitty, which is taken by the player that gets the first trick," Grandma explained. "After the cards are dealt out, we pass three of our cards to the player on the right. The next time, we pass left, and the third time we pass across. The player with the two of clubs starts the game. The object is to not take any tricks with hearts or the queen of spades in them. Hearts count one point each, and the queen counts thirteen points. When one player's score gets to fifty, the player with the least points wins. If a player takes all the points, they have 'shot the moon,' which means that all the other players get twenty-six points. Any questions?"

All was quiet.

"Let's play!" Basil said as he began to deal out the cards.

The game became noisy every time someone took the queen of spades—it was always fun to dump the queen on someone else.

After much laughter, screaming, and dumping of the queen, the game ended, with Denny as the winner. He was very pleased with himself, because he seldom won at card games.

*   *   *

Bong! Bong! Bong! The large grandfather clock struck twelve times.

"Oh my goodness! It's twelve already. Where has the evening gone?" Hannah lamented.

"What fun we had," Basil said. "Thank you all for the wonderful time."

Basil put his arm around Hannah's back. "We'd better go to sleep, old girl," he said. "Chores to do in the morning—Christmas Day or not."

"Yes," Hannah agreed. "I'll have to be up early to put the Christmas goose into the oven. I've made the stuffing, so it won't take too long."

"Come on, Abby; I'm ready to hit the hay," Grandpa said as he started for the stairway that led to his bedroom on the second floor.

"I'll be right up," Abby said. She started picking up some food plates that remained on the table. "I'll clean up the food and plates—then I'll come to bed. You children are excused. Don't stay up too late playing with your gifts. Tomorrow is another day."

The tired children headed for their bedrooms.

"That was fun," Missy said and smiled. "It's more fun with lots of people around."

"Yeah," Randy agreed. "We usually have only Grandma, Grandpa, and Dad around on Christmas Eve. It's not very exciting at home."

Jenny put her arms around Missy's shoulders. "Yeah, it was fun, and we've got another week after Christmas to have more fun. Come on, we'll have to get to sleep fast. I can't wait until morning."

It's too late to have a Peanut Butter Club meeting tonight, Audrey thought. *I'll have to wait until morning to tell them about my visit to old man Moses's cabin.*

Chapter 12

Spying on Christmas Day

"It happened again!" Basil stormed as he stomped into the kitchen on Christmas morning.

"Shusssh! Not so loud." Hannah covered his mouth with her hand. "You'll wake the others."

"Sorry—but I'm mad. That creature was in the dog barn last night and stole one of Babe's puppies! The brown-and-cream-colored one. He also made a mess by dumping dog food all over the place."

"What about a cream-and-brown puppy?" Audrey asked while rubbing the sleep out of her eyes as she entered the kitchen.

"One of Babe's puppies was taken last night," Hannah said in a matter-of-fact tone of voice as she continued to put stuffing into the goose.

"Not Peanut!" Audrey exclaimed in horror.

"I didn't know she had a name." Basil looked surprised.

"We gave her a name—we girls did. We love her. Is she the one that is gone?" Audrey wailed.

"I'm afraid so," Basil said sadly. "Something broke into the dog barn and made a mess last night. Now the puppy is gone, and the food is scattered all over the place. Even the electric heater was turned off. It's a good thing it wasn't so cold last night or Delilah's puppies would have frozen to death."

"That's awful," Audrey cried. "That creature has no sense of fair play—picking on defenseless puppies. He has no heart. If he'd picked on Buster, he'd be dead meat by now."

"That could be true," Basil said. "Whoever it was must have fed the adult dogs some fancy treats so they wouldn't cause a fuss. It must have happened while we were in church last night. I didn't go out to check the dogs before bed the way I usually do, because it was so late when we went to bed. I should have done it anyway," Basil lamented.

"Now, now," Hannah said to comfort her husband. "There wasn't much you could have done in the middle of the night."

"That's true," Basil agreed. "I'll have to call Sheriff Miller and report this. No more Mr. Nice Guy—this creature is starting to tick me off!"

"After breakfast," Hannah suggested. "We don't want to get the poor sheriff out of bed on Christmas morning. Besides, the harm has already been done, so we might as well enjoy Christmas and take this up tomorrow."

"We'll destroy the crime scene by tomorrow," Basil said. "I'll have to call this in soon, so Sheriff Miller can start the investigation."

"If you insist," Hannah said with a shrug. "I've got a Christmas dinner to prepare, so everyone gets cereal and toast this morning. It's on the kitchen table if anyone is interested."

While Basil sat down to breakfast, Audrey ran back to her bedroom in the hunters' lodge.

"Wake up, everyone!" she shouted as she ran down the hall and banged on the boys' bedroom door. Then she ran into the girls' bedroom.

"Peanut's gone!" she shouted as she entered the girls' bedroom. "Everyone get up!"

"Are you crazy or something?" Jenny said, still half asleep. "Why are you running and shouting so early in the morning?"

"It's not early. It's almost eight o'clock. Get up—this is an emergency—there's been a theft. A puppy has been stolen, and the barn has been vandalized!"

"What?" Missy said as she yawned. "Who did that?"

"We don't know—that's the mystery. It seems to be another of Bigfoot's doings," Audrey answered. "That creature has no heart. He steals puppies and destroys dog food—what a heartless beast!"

"When did this happen?" Jenny demanded as she crawled out of bed and started putting on her new blue jeans.

The boys, in their pajamas, burst through the door, followed by Laddie, who was barking excitedly. It seemed they were having a group panic attack.

Missy ran for the bathroom with her clothes, yelling, "Stay out of our room, you sneaky boys—we're not dressed."

Jenny grabbed a sweatshirt and ran for the closet. Then she stumbled, her blue jeans falling down around her knees.

The boys began to laugh hysterically. Laddie barked uncontrollably—he was caught up in the excitement.

Audrey stood in the middle of the room with a look of horror written all over her face. *Good grief,* she thought. *This is no way to respond to an emergency.* "Chill out, everybody!" she shouted while grabbing Laddie and trying to quiet him down.

When the noise had lessened somewhat, Audrey related to the boys what Basil had told her earlier. After Jenny and Missy were dressed, Audrey suggested they have a Peanut Butter Club meeting, to make plans and get organized. "We need to get on this right away, before the sheriff gets here. We need to find some clues and make some plans. The sheriff may insist we stay out of this, and we don't want to cross the sheriff."

The group sat down on the big braided rug in the middle of the room. They went through the opening gestures, and Audrey started the meeting by telling the group what she had seen at Jebediah Moses's cabin the day before. "There is more than one person living there, I'm sure. From the looks of the fancy cowboy boots I saw, that person is much younger than old man Moses. There were two empty cups on the table, and I smelled coffee in the room. This could mean that the other person is old enough to drink coffee. The old man didn't want us in the cabin and was very anxious for us to leave—which all seems very suspicious to me."

"I think you're right," Randy agreed.

"And also," Audrey continued, "when Hannah asked him why he had cleared so many trees lately, he said he needed more firewood. I didn't see a lot of firewood stacked up outside. There was a small pile of wood on the porch, and there was a small, old shed out back that could have been full of firewood. I think someone is selling that wood—maybe illegally. I don't think you can go out into government parks or forests and chop down wood to sell it. Maybe we should ask the sheriff about that when he gets here today."

"Good idea," Jenny said.

"Maybe that nephew of his—Mason, I think is what Hannah called him—is already there," Denny surmised. "Maybe he's the one cutting down the trees. If the old man is as old as you say he is, he can't cut down trees anymore—at least not without help."

"These are all good deductions," Audrey said to compliment the group. "But why does a young person need all that money when he's living with someone else?"

"Didn't Basil say that Mason was a worthless person who never did any work? Maybe he sells wood and steals puppies to get money for an addiction," Randy said in a matter-of-fact way. "I know people who do that."

"Now we're getting someplace," Audrey said. "Now we've got a motive for the crimes, but we still don't know why this person is dressing up like Bigfoot and trying to make life hard for Basil and Hannah. They have been very kind to Jeb."

"That's true," Missy said softly, "but sometimes people will bite the hand that feeds them. I've heard my Grandpa Elmer talk about such people. They don't want to feel obligated, so they back-stab the very people that help them."

"That is so profound, Missy," Audrey said with amazement. "You may be quiet, but you sure come up with some great thoughts at times."

"I listen and think," Missy said with a smile. "I only give my opinion when I've got something important to say."

The group decided to have breakfast, go out to the barns and help clean up, and then look for clues before the sheriff came.

At the breakfast table, Basil put the kibosh on their plans. "The sheriff said not to touch anything in the barns until he gets here."

"Can we go into the woods, then?" Denny asked.

Basil looked at Hannah for an answer to Denny's question.

"I guess that would be okay—just be back by noon," Hannah said, with a stern look the children knew only too well.

"I've got a big goose and lots of good things to eat cooking, and I want some big appetites here at the table—on time!"

* * *

"These tracks are human footprints," Randy said. He was examining the fresh tracks behind the barn that led across the lake and into the woods.

"Yes," Audrey agreed. "And they are going down the same path Hannah and I took to the Moses place. I'll bet they end there too."

The children ran along the ski path, and a half-hour later they were near the Moses cabin. Smoke was coming out of the chimney.

"Let's scatter and surround the cabin," Denny suggested. "We'll spy on them from all sides."

"Okay," Randy agreed. "Denny and I will go west, around the back of the cabin; Jenny and Missy can go east; and Audrey and Ty can stay here at our starting point. Remember, we all need to come back here!"

The group surrounded the cabin and watched. They staked out the place for half an hour and didn't see anyone leave the cabin. Things remained peaceful and quiet.

"We'd better get back," Audrey said to Ty after forty minutes had passed. "Hannah will get mad if we're late for Christmas dinner. You stay here, and I'll get the others."

"Okay," Ty said. He was busy picking up pine cones from beneath the large evergreen trees and stuffing them inside the front of his coat. "I'm going to build something with these when I get home."

"Good for you," Audrey said with a smile. "Now, stay in this area, and don't get lost. Okay?"

"Okay,"

Denny and Randy spying

"I can see light in that window," Denny whispered, while peeking out from behind a snow-covered evergreen where he and Randy were watching the back of the cabin.

"So can I," Randy whispered back. "There hasn't been much movement inside."

"Not yet. Maybe they sleep late," Denny surmised.

"Maybe—wait! I see someone at the window—look out!"

Both boys ducked behind the evergreen.

"Do you think they saw us?" Randy whispered.

"Naw, I don't think so. They'd come outside if they did."

The boys waited. They didn't hear any doors open or slam shut, so they assumed they were safe.

After a few minutes, Denny peeked again. "Someone is cooking something by the stove," he said.

"Must be Jeb," Randy said.

"Wait. Now there is another person standing by the stove," Denny said excitedly. "We caught them! There are two of them inside."

"Not so loud," Randy said, and he put his hand over Denny's mouth. When he took his hand away, he said, "Good spy job, Denny. At least we know Mason, or someone else, is there. We can tell the sheriff that. We'd better get out of here before they hear us."

The boys started back to where Audrey and Ty were waiting. They moved slowly and carefully, crouching down so they wouldn't be seen, until they were away from the cabin.

They met Audrey sneaking through the trees about halfway back to the starting point.

"Where are you going?" Denny whispered.

"To find you guys," Audrey replied.

"Well, we're coming to you, so head on back," Randy informed her. "We'll tell you what we saw when we all get back to our starting point."

When the three arrived at the starting point, there was no Ty in sight.

"Oh, good grief!" Audrey said disgustedly. "I told him to stay here. I'll go get Jenny and Missy, before they get lost. You guys see if you can find some tracks that Ty might have left in the snow."

Audrey found Jenny and Missy behind some scrubs near the cabin; they were whispering to each other and giggling softly.

Audrey sneaked up to them and whispered, "Let's go."

Jenny and Missy jumped and Jenny started to scream, but Audrey cupped her hand over Jenny's mouth.

"Stop that!" Audrey whispered. "You'll give us away."

The three girls ran into the woods to hide, in case someone had heard the scream and came out of the cabin looking for them.

*　　*　　*

The cabin door opened slowly. Old man Moses stuck his head out and looked around. He didn't see anything, so he pulled his head back inside and closed the door.

"That must have been a screech owl," he said to Mason. "Let's have breakfast, and then we'll go out and investigate."

Chapter 13

Spotting Bigfoot

"What in the world was so funny back there?" Audrey asked when the girls were safely out of sight and sound of the cabin.

"We saw two men in the cabin—in long red underwear!" Jenny giggled. Missy covered her mouth with her hand and giggled softly.

"What's so funny about that?" Audrey questioned. "Lots of people sleep in their underwear."

"Long red underwear?" Jenny questioned, raising her eyebrows.

"Whatever!" Audrey put an end to the ridiculous discussion. "We need to get back to the starting point and find Ty. He's disappeared, after I told him to stay put."

*   *   *

"Ty, where are you?" Randy called. He was following some fresh tracks to a large evergreen with low-hanging boughs covered with snow.

"I'm here." A small, frightened voice came from under the tree.

Denny fell to the ground in front of the tree and crawled under it, to find Ty all curled up against the trunk.

"What are you doing under here, squirt?" Denny asked.

"I'm hiding," Ty answered in a whisper; his voice quivered.

"Why?"

"Bigfoot is out there."

"How do you know that?"

"I saw him," Ty said, trembling all over.

Randy had crawled under the tree in time to hear Ty say he'd seen Bigfoot.

"Where did you see him?" Randy asked.

"Here—next to this tree—just a few minutes after Audrey left to find you guys. I crawled under here to pick up some big pine cones, and when I was getting ready to leave, two hairy feet walked by. I froze and waited for a few minutes; then I peeked out from under the tree and saw the monster getting ready to sit down on that rock over there." Ty pointed to a large bolder about five yards from the tree.

"After I saw him, I decided to stay under the tree," Ty said matter-of-factly.

"Good plan, pal," Randy complimented Ty as they all crawled out from under the tree. "Can you tell us what he looked like?"

"He was big and hairy—like a funny-looking ape. He was scary!" Ty shuddered.

"Too bad you didn't have a camera," Denny said. "You could have taken a picture and we'd have proof that he exists."

"I can draw a picture when I get home," Ty volunteered. "I'm a good drawer."

"I'll bet!" Denny said sarcastically.

Just then the girls came into view. Denny and Randy told them Ty's story.

Audrey's mouth dropped open with horror and shock. "He was probably following us out here today," she said. "If something had happened to you, Ty, I never would have forgiven myself." She hugged her little brother tightly.

Jenny looked frightened as she glanced around. "Maybe he's still here."

Missy's eyes opened wide and a frightened look came over her face. She stood frozen, glancing from side to side.

"I can draw a picture of him," Ty volunteered again.

"What good would that do?" Jenny asked.

"Ty's a pretty good drawer—if I say so myself," Audrey said. "He can draw a picture and give us a good profile of the creature. That will help us find him, if we know what we are looking for."

A light went on in Jenny's brain. "If Ty did see Bigfoot, and we saw Jeb and Mason in the cabin, that means Jeb and Mason could not be Bigfoot. Bigfoot must be a real creature," she said excitedly.

"Or maybe someone else is pretending to be Bigfoot," Audrey said. "This is getting more and more complicated."

The children hurried back to the Husky Hideaway, glancing from side to side as they ran through the forest. They had agreed to tell their story to the sheriff when he got to the Husky Lodge.

*   *   *

Upon arrival at the lodge, the children saw a police car with the words Sheriff Miller written on its side.

"He's here!" Denny said breathlessly as they passed the car.

"Let's go inside and tell him what we found out," Audrey suggested.

The children burst into the kitchen excitedly; they all wanted to be the first one to tell their story. The adults were sitting around the kitchen table having coffee. The children all began talking at the same time.

"Stop right there!" Grandma ordered over the noise. "Take off your boots before you come into this kitchen."

"Ty saw Bigfoot!" Audrey shouted over the noise, as she sat down on the kitchen floor to take off her snow boots.

"What?" Basil asked. "Talk one at a time, so we can hear you."

"Ty, you tell it," Audrey suggested when everyone had become quiet.

"I saw Bigfoot, while I was hiding under a tree," Ty said proudly.

"What!" Grandma gasped. She began to fire one question after another at the group. "Where were the rest of you? Why did you leave Ty alone? What were you doing under a tree, Ty?"

"We were spying on Jeb's cabin," Audrey replied.

"Why?" Grandpa Josh demanded.

"Because the tracks behind the barn led down the ski path to Jeb's cabin," Audrey replied.

"Were these the tracks of the person that stole the puppy?" asked Sheriff Miller.

"We think so," Randy chimed in. "The tracks were fresh and led from the barn, across the lake, and into the woods. They were human tracks—not Bigfoot's tracks."

"Okay," the sheriff said calmly. "Now tell me, did you find the puppy?"

"No, but—we spied on Jeb and found out that there were two men in the cabin. Jeb had a visitor," Randy explained.

"What's wrong with that?" asked the sheriff.

"Well, yesterday when Hannah and I were there, Jeb acted funny and didn't mention a visitor," Audrey explained. "He was trying to hide something."

"Go on," the sheriff encouraged Audrey.

"Well, there is a lot of timber being cleared around the cabin and in different parts of the forest near the cabin," Audrey explained. "Jeb said he needed lots of wood, but we didn't see a lot of woodpiles around the place."

"So?" the sheriff questioned.

"So is it legal to cut down trees in a state forest and sell them?" Audrey questioned.

"No!" the sheriff responded forcefully. "Only fallen trees and dead branches can be removed from the forest for burning. I'll have to have a talk with Jeb about that. Anything else?"

"Well, since we saw Bigfoot and Jeb and his guest at the same time, we know that Jeb and his guest aren't Bigfoot," Jenny said proudly.

"Good deduction, young lady." The sheriff grinned. "Now, how do I know this young boy saw Bigfoot? He could have imagined the whole thing."

"I can draw a picture," Ty said defiantly, after having remained quiet throughout the discussion.

"Oh, you can?" the sheriff said with a chuckle.

"If he can draw a good picture of Bigfoot, that should prove he saw something, since he's never seen Bigfoot before," Audrey said.

"That's true," the sheriff agreed. "Okay, Ty—go draw a picture while I finish my coffee; then Basil and I will go out to Jeb's cabin and see what's been going on out there."

The children went into the great room and sat around the big oak table while Ty drew his picture.

"Wow—that's scary," Jenny said when she saw the finished product. "Are you sure you saw that creature, or are you making this all up?"

"I saw him!" Ty replied forcefully.

"He was so scared that a permanent picture of the monster may have been burned into his memory—forever," Audrey speculated. "I just hope he doesn't have nightmares over this."

"When we find out who this monster really is, Ty will see that it's only a joke someone is playing, and he won't be afraid anymore," Missy assured the group as she gave Ty a big hug.

Ty's drawing of Bigfoot

*   *   *

After breakfast, Jeb and Mason were cleaning up the dishes when they heard a yipping sound coming from the direction of Mason's bedroom.

"What's that?" Jeb asked with a surprised look on his face.

"It must be coming from outside. Maybe it's a coyote near the house," Mason suggested.

"I doubt that!" Jeb said as he headed for Mason's bedroom and opened the door. Peanut came running out, yipping happily because she had been set free.

"What's this?" Jeb asked Mason.

"A puppy I bought yesterday."

"Where?"

"From Basil."

"When?"

"About seven last night, when I went out for a walk."

"Oh. What did you pay?"

"One hundred dollars."

Jeb looked at Mason skeptically. Then he went back to cleaning up the kitchen.

"I'll go outside and bring in some wood," Mason volunteered. He put on his coat and snow boots and went outside, taking Peanut with him. Later, when Mason returned with the wood, he no long had Peanut with him.

"Where's the puppy?" Jeb asked

"She ran away when I put her down to potty," Mason replied.

"She'll freeze to death out there in the forest all by herself," Jeb said with a scowl on his face.

"Too bad!" Mason replied. "She shouldn't have run away."

"That's a hundred dollars wasted," Jeb said. "Either you are a fool, or you didn't buy that puppy. I'll bet you stole it."

Mason stormed out of the cabin without replying to Jeb's remark.

*   *   *

An hour later, the sheriff and Basil showed up at the cabin on Basil's snowmobile. They knocked at the door.

Jeb answered the door with a scowl on his face. "What do you want?" he snarled.

"We need to ask you some questions," Sheriff Miller said. "Can we come in?"

"Suit yourselves!" Jeb stepped back from the door to allow the sheriff and Basil to enter the cabin.

After the three were seated around the table having coffee, the sheriff said, "Basil had one of his puppies taken last night between seven and nine o'clock. Do you know anything about this?"

"No!" Jeb answered sharply.

"How about your guest?" Basil asked.

"He's gone—left about an hour ago. I don't know where he went!" Jeb snapped.

"Don't bite my head off," Basil said calmly. "You know if that puppy is left out in the woods, she'll die. Come on, Jeb, tell us what happened."

Jeb sat sullenly quiet.

"Jeb, you'll be an accessory to the crime if you don't help us," the sheriff said.

Jeb sat quietly looking down at the table.

All three men remained quiet for a long time.

"I'm sorry about this, Jeb," Basil said. "We've been friends for a long time. If your nephew is up to no good, you'd better get him some help. A small crime can lead to a bigger crime, you know."

Jeb sat quietly twitching in his chair and rubbing his hands together. He seemed nervous, but he wouldn't say a word.

The sheriff broke the silence. "By the way—do you know anything about all the trees that have been cut down around here?"

"They were all dead. Some kind of tree disease," Jeb answered quickly. "I used them for firewood."

"Why is this tree disease only killing trees around your cabin?" the sheriff asked.

"I don't know!" Jeb snapped back. "I'm busy—got things to do. If you two have anything to do on Christmas Day besides accuse a neighbor of wrongdoing—then go do it."

Jeb got up and opened the cabin door, indicating he wanted his guests to leave. The sheriff and Basil got up and headed for the door.

"I'll be back with help," the sheriff said. "This isn't over!"

*   *   *

"Did you find Peanut?" Audrey asked nervously when she saw Basil enter the kitchen door without the puppy.

"No, but we're pretty sure they took the puppy. I don't think Jeb took it, but he knows who did."

Audrey hung her head as tears welled up in her eyes. *What will become of poor Peanut?* she thought.

"It's time to eat," Hannah said softly. "Get everyone in here. Dinner has been ready for over an hour."

*   *   *

The children were sad when they heard that Basil hadn't found Peanut. They were all very hungry too after their morning of sleuthing in the forest, so they ate heartily, in silence, until all that was left on the table was some bones and meat scraps from the goose.

"I'm stuffed," Grandpa said, rubbing his tummy. "Excellent meal, Hannah. Thanks. I think I'll go take a nap."

"Sounds good," Basil agreed.

Just then, the group heard a scratching at the front door, followed by the howling of a wolf in the distance.

Denny ran to the door and opened it. In burst Peanut—yipping and sniffing around for food.

Missy grabbed her, sat down on the floor, and hugged the happy puppy close to her chest, while the other children gathered around to pet the puppy. Everyone was overjoyed to see Peanut.

"I wonder how she found her way home?" Basil looked puzzled. "Puppies this young usually don't have a good sense of direction."

"That wolf cry—check outside for a wolf," Hannah suggested.

The whole family ran out to the porch just in time to see a big black wolf run across the lake and into the woods.

"That's Chico," Randy shouted. "He brought Peanut home, just like he brought Denny and me home during the storm."

"He's one smart wolf," Denny said with a big grin on his face.

"Get the table scraps," Hannah ordered, "and put them outside on the ski path that leads into the forest. Chico deserves a good Christmas dinner for saving Peanut's life."

Missy hugging Peanut

Chapter 14

Learning to Be a Musher

"Today we'll hitch the dogs to the sled and go for a ride," Basil announced at the breakfast table the day after Christmas.

"Yay!" all the children shouted at once, while Grandpa covered his ears.

"Shush!" Audrey said, pointing at Grandpa.

The children became quiet and started eating as fast as they could. After breakfast the rush was on to see who could get outside first to help hitch up the dogs.

Morning chores were done first, and then Basil instructed the children to put sock-like booties on seven of the dogs. Next he explained that the booties protected the dogs' feet from web cracks. "If we don't have dogs wear booties, the snow and ice will ball up under their paws and cause sores—then they can't pull a sled," Basil said.

Next, the X-back harnesses were put on each dog so they could be hitched up to the large sled.

"Buster is the lead dog," Basil explained. "He'll be out in front. Behind him we have Eddy and Andy; they are called the swing dogs. Behind the swing dogs, we have Stella and Mabel; they are called the team dogs, and the two dogs closest to the sled are the wheel dogs, Cody and Nick—one big, happy family. They all love to run. Huskies are born to run."

The dogs were next hooked to the towline, the long rope running down the middle of the dog team. They were attached by their harnesses so they couldn't turn around and get the team tangled up.

After the dogs were hooked up, they seemed anxious to go. They pulled on the towline and started to bark and jump with excitement.

Basil instructed the three boys to get into the sled, while he stepped onto the sled runners—the two bottom pieces of the sled that would slide across the snow.

Basil grabbed the handlebar of the sled and shouted, "Line out!" to get the team straightened out in front of the sled. Then he shouted, "Mush! Hike!"

The dogs took off like a shot from a gun. The boys grabbed the sides of the sled as they fell backward into the sled. They hung on for dear life while laughing hysterically.

Basil aimed the sled for the lake—running behind to make the sled lighter. When the dogs were in full stride, racing along the ski trail, Basil shouted over the cold wind, "We're going about fifteen miles an hour!"

"It feels faster," Denny shouted back, as the cold wind stole his breath away.

"My tears are freezing to my cheeks," Ty wailed, trying to brush the tears off his face.

The sled zipped along the trail, making a whooshing sound. The bright sun reflecting off the white snow made it hard to see.

"Yippee!" Randy shouted, enjoying every minute of the ride. "How do you turn this thing or stop it?" he shouted, turning to look at Basil.

"You turn it by leaning on the runners—like downhill skiing—after you shout the right commands to the dogs. I'll demonstrate later," Basil assured Randy.

After a half-mile run, Basil slowed the dogs down a bit. He then shouted "Come haw!" and turned the team left so they could cross the lake. Buster, the lead dog, was the one that obeyed all the commands and guided the team.

When the sled was on the other side of the lake, Basil shouted, "Come gee!" and the team turned right and followed the ski trail into the woods.

The beautiful snow-covered evergreens raced by while the sun shone brightly through the trees on either side of the trail.

As the team traveled deeper into the woods, it was getting darker and the trail narrower.

"We won't run into any grizzly bears out here, will we?" Ty asked.

"No bears." Basil said with a laugh. "They are all hibernating this time of year."

"What's hibernating?" Ty wondered out loud.

"Sleeping, pinhead!" Denny replied.

"We might run into a moose, though," Basil said. "If a dogsled surprises a moose on the trail, he can get pretty touchy. Sometimes a mother moose will protect her young one by charging the sled and dogs. That can get ugly."

During the trip Basil would shout different commands—like "Tshckt" (keep going), "Trail" (yield the right of way), and "Go by" (pay no attention to a distraction)—at the team, and they would follow his orders—led by Buster.

When the team and riders returned home, Basil shouted the word Ty had been waiting to hear: "Whoa!" The team stopped, and the passengers got out of the sled. Ty had enjoyed the ride but was half frozen, so he raced for the house to get warmed up.

The girls got to ride next. Basil took the same trail and explained the same terms to the girls as he had to the boys. He wanted all the children to learn how to be good mushers.

"Who wants to be a musher?" Basil asked when everyone had gotten a ride.

"I do!" all the children shouted, and they jumped with excitement.

"Okay, we'll start with the oldest, Audrey. Who wants to ride along?" Basil asked. No one volunteered.

"Oh, come on! I'll be running right behind her. We won't go too fast," Basil said.

Missy and Jenny climbed into the sled. They thought they had better ride with Audrey if they expected her to ride with them.

One by one the children learned to be mushers. Basil made the trips short and kept the dogs from running too fast. Each child had to learn the different commands and how to lean on the runners. By lunchtime they were all experienced mushers.

*　　*　　*

"Do you think Laddie could learn to be a sled dog?" Ty asked between slurps of his chicken noodle soup at the lunchtime meal.

"I don't know if that old dog can learn any new tricks," Grandma answered. "He might have a heart attack."

"I'll tell you what, young man," Basil said. "We have a small sled and a one-dog harness that our son, Brad, used to drive when he was about your age. I'll dig it out, and we'll hitch old Laddie to that sled and see what he can do."

"Whoopee!" Ty yelled jumping up from the table. "I'll get ready!"

"You'll finish your lunch first!" Grandma said, grabbing Ty by the seat of his pants and pulling him back into his chair.

*　　*　　*

The children helped hitch Laddie to the old sled. Ty got on the runners, grabbed the handlebar, and shouted, "Mush! Hike!"

Laddie stood still. Then he turned around in his harness, looked at Ty with disgust, and lay down in the snow.

"I think he needs some encouragement," Basil said and laughed. Basil took hold of the harness and pulled on it. "Come on, Laddie," he encouraged the old dog. "Let's go for a walk."

Laddie tried to move, but the sled stopped him, and he lay down again.

"Let me try!" Ty said, walking to the front of the sled and taking hold of the harness. Laddie moved along with Ty but stopped the minute the boy stopped.

"You get back on the sled," Grandpa Josh instructed. "I'll see if I can get this old dog to move. Grandpa Josh got down beside Laddie on his hands and knees. "Now, you shout Mush! Hike!" he told Ty.

When Ty shouted the command, Grandpa started moving the sled and Laddie at the same time. When Ty shouted "Whoa," Grandpa stopped, and so did Laddie. They repeated this procedure several times.

Grandpa let go of the harness and got up. He brushed off his knees and said, "Now, try it again."

"Mush! Hike!" Ty shouted. Laddie took off slowly but steadily. After about a hundred yards, Laddie lay down to rest.

Ty took a doggie treat out of his pocket and fed it to Laddie. "Good dog," he said. "We'll try this again tomorrow, after you've rested."

Ty unhitched the old dog and took him to the house to lie in front of the fireplace.

* * *

Sheriff Miller showed up at the Husky Hideaway about three o'clock. Hannah invited him in for coffee.

"Well, what did you find out?" Basil asked as the sheriff sipped coffee.

The sheriff seemed in no hurry to tell what he knew about the mystery at the Moses cabin.

"I went back to Jeb's today, after getting a warrant to search the place, so Jeb decided to confess rather than have his place searched." The sheriff spoke slowly and paused a moment before continuing his story.

"It's seems that Mason has been staying with Jeb for some time but has now disappeared. Mason also was the one who cut down all the trees and sold the lumber. I guess Mason likes to smoke marijuana, and that costs money. That may be the reason he stole the puppy too."

"The puppy came back last night," Basil said.

"That's strange." The sheriff looked surprised. "Most small puppies wouldn't know their way home."

"I thought that too," Basil said. "It seems like a wolf found the puppy wandering in the woods and brought her home."

"Well, I'll be danged!" the sheriff exclaimed. He paused a moment and added, "Do you want to press charges?"

"No, but I'd like to talk to Mason when you find him. That young man is headed for a whole lot of trouble if he doesn't straighten up soon."

"I agree with that," the sheriff said as he took the last sip of coffee and got up from the table. "Keep me informed if you find out anything else, okay?" He put on his hat and headed for the door.

"Okay. Thanks for dropping over and letting us know about everything." Basil patted the sheriff on the back as he walked him to the door.

* * *

The Peanut Butter Club met before bedtime that night. Audrey told the others about the conversation she had overheard between the sheriff and Basil.

"Well, that tells us who took the puppy and is selling illegal wood—but why would Mason want to vandalize the woodpile, steal Christmas lights, and cause trouble for Hannah and Basil?" Randy asked.

"It doesn't make sense, unless he's doing that stuff and getting paid for his dirty work by someone else," Jenny surmised.

Audrey complimented the group: "Good deductions. The next question is: Who in the neighborhood wants to cause trouble for Basil and Hannah, and why?"

"We'll have to ask Hannah and Basil that question in the morning," suggested Denny. "I'm tired. It's been a fun day of mushing—let's go to bed."

"All in favor say "I" said Audrey.

"I," the children responded in unison. Even Laddie barked and took off for the boys' bedroom. He was tired after pulling that heavy sled and trying to figure out all those order he'd been given.

Hannah making pancakes

Chapter 15

The Plot Thickens

"Is there anyone around here that wants to do you and Basil harm?" Denny asked Hannah as she filled his plate with freshly made pancakes.

"Where did that come from?" Hannah laughed as she looked with surprise at Denny.

"Nice going, pinhead!" Jenny mumbled, her mouth full of pancakes.

"That wasn't too diplomatic, Denny," Grandma explained. "You shouldn't ask Hannah personal questions that are none of your business."

"I only wanted to help," Denny replied, hanging his head in shame and focusing on his pancakes.

Basil smiled at the dejected boy. "It's all right, Denny. We know your heart is in the right place." He paused a moment. "Well now, let me think. We have a neighbor named Ralph Redland that isn't too happy with me because I win the Northern Lights Sled Dog Race every year. I think he'd like to see me leave."

"I don't know," Hannah chimed in. "Ralph can be grouchy and competitive at the dog races, but he's not such a bad sort. When we moved in here ten years ago, he gave you lots of good advice on how to run this place."

Basil laughed. "I don't know how good his advice was. We seem to be going into debt more each year."

"That's not Ralph's fault." Hannah defended their neighbor.

"I'm sorry to hear about your financial problems," Grandma said. "Maybe Josh and I could help."

"That's really nice of you," Basil said and smiled, "but we can handle this. I've got a yearly payment coming up in January, and if I win the Northern Lights race, we'll have enough to cover that debt and have some left over for some improvements around here and to buy more dog food."

"That's part of the problem," Hannah said. "Those dogs eat a lot and bring in little or no income."

She paused a moment and then continued her discussion in a casual manner, as if her comment wasn't too important. "I guess we should have sold this place to that lumber company that was here last summer and offered us a very good price for this lodge."

"What lumber company?" Audrey perked up, wanting to extract more information from Hannah.

"That lumber company that's trying to buy up all the land around here to provide wood for their mill in Duluth," Hannah answered. "I think their name was the Great Lakes Lumber Mill."

"Oh, yeah." Basil joined the conversation. "I remember that now. They went around to all the neighbors. It seems that the government land around here has gotten some new restrictions on how to cut and harvest lumber—environmentalists' doings—so this mill wants to buy enough private property to set up their own mill here. Some of the neighbors wanted to sell. I think Ralph did, but Hannah and I like this place just the way it is."

"Where would all the animals go if you cut down their homes?" Ty asked sadly.

"I guess they'd all have to live in the government-owned forests," Grandma replied.

"We'll just have to win that race, so we won't have to sell this place. Then the animals can all stay here and be happy," Basil assured Ty with a determined nod of his head.

"That sounds good." Hannah smiled. "Now, everyone finish your breakfasts so you can go out and practice, practice, practice racing the dogs. Sitting here eating won't win any races!"

*   *   *

The children, Basil, and Grandpa bustled around feeding the dogs, chopping wood, and shoveling snow. When the chores were done, they all worked together to hitch the dogs to the sled to practice racing.

"We'll let the boys help with the racing this morning and the girls can exercise the other dogs that aren't racing," Basil suggested. "We'll switch around tomorrow."

"Can I hook Laddie up to his sled and work with him?" Ty asked.

"Sure," Basil answered. "Randy, Denny and I will run the team."

"I'll try to help Ty," Grandpa Josh volunteered.

"Thanks, Grandpa," Ty yelled as he raced to the shed to get out the small sled and single harness. Laddie raced along at Ty's heels, barking with excitement.

After Laddie was all hooked up, Grandpa suggested Ty run along behind the sled to make the load lighter for the old dog. This seemed to work out well, because Laddie could handle the weight of the sled nicely. The happy pair ran merrily down the trail, laughing and barking.

"Don't go too far!" Grandpa shouted as the boy and dog headed for the lake.

Ty shouted some commands at Laddie, but the old dog did whatever he wanted to do—running here and there and almost upsetting the sled now and then.

Ty got tired of running, so he jumped onto the runners of the sled and shouted, "Whoa!"

The extra weight on the sled tightened the harness and stopped the dog so quickly that Ty almost tumbled over. Both the boy and the dog were now winded.

"We'll rest awhile, Laddie," Ty said, petting the old dog between his ears. Both sat down in the snow at the edge of the lake and looked into the dense, dark forest ahead of them.

"I don't think we'll go into the woods today," Ty said to Laddie. "It's scary in there."

Laddie lay panting in the snow, not taking much note of the boy's statement.

After they had rested, they got up, Ty turned Laddie and the sled around by hand, and the tired twosome headed back to Husky Hideaway.

*   *   *

"You two are really going to be good mushers," Basil said to compliment the boys when they'd returned from the practice runs.

"Thanks," Denny and Randy said in unison.

"I really like this," Denny bubbled. "I didn't know dogsled racing could be so much fun."

"It's more fun than snowmobiling," Randy said with a grin. "At least the dogs don't break down and have to be pushed home."

Everyone laughed.

"Well," Basil said, "you've got to feed the dogs and not run them too far or fast. If you abuse your dogs, they can break down too."

"We'd never do that," Denny assured Basil.

"Good!" Basil smiled and then added, "That race we're entering this weekend will be eighty miles long. It's about five hours of full-out running. To be good mushers, you two have to learn to run along behind the sled, so you'd better practice running too. You can get in about a mile of cross-country running before lunch."

Basil turned and looked at the boys, who weren't moving. "Goodbye. I'll put the dogs away," he said with a grin.

Randy and Denny stood looking at each other for a few seconds, while Basil started unhooking the dogs from the sled.

"Come on, Denny." Randy poked Denny's arm with his fist. "Let's get going."

"Stay on the road, so you don't get lost," Basil shouted as the boys took off. Then he laughed loudly as he unhitched the dogs.

*   *   *

Basil noticed a car in front of the lodge when he approached the house. *Maybe we've got a paying guest,* he thought.

Upon entering the kitchen, he noticed Jeb and Mason seated at the big table, having coffee and rolls.

"Mason has come to apologize," Hannah said when Basil sat down at the table.

"Oh?" Basil looked at Mason.

"I'm sorry I took your puppy," Mason mumbled.

"Speak up, boy!" Jeb poked Mason's arm.

"I'm sorry," Mason said again, louder.

"I'm sorry too," Basil said. "I'm especially sorry that you are ruining your life with your marijuana habit. You've got to get off that stuff!"

"I know," Mason said meekly.

There was a moment of silence as the three men thought about what to say next.

Jeb spoke first. "Mason will have to go to court for the wood stealing, but the lawyer said he'd probably only get probation on that."

"I'd like to ask you a question." Basil looked at Mason.

"Okay."

"Were you the one that messed up my woodpiles and stole the Christmas-tree lights?"

"No, sir!" Mason answered emphatically.

Basil looked intensely at Mason, "Good. I'd hate to see you arrested for vandalism."

Mason hung his head and looked at the table. Basil couldn't tell whether Mason was lying. *Time will tell,* Basil thought.

Chapter 16

A Moose on the Loose

The next two days went by quickly. They ran the dog sled team in the morning for about two hours and in the afternoon for about four hours. The dogs were getting stronger and more confident.

The boys and girls would be out running behind the sled when they weren't taking their turn as the head musher. The adults thought this plan was working out great. By bedtime the children were all tired out and didn't fuss about having to go to sleep.

As the noisy parade of dogs, sled, and children raced through the woods, the snow rabbits, raccoons, and deer all ran for cover. The animals didn't want to get run over by the zealous group.

After all the practice sessions, the group talked excitedly about winning the big race on Saturday.

Ty intently worked with Laddie, trying to teach him the art of being a good sled dog. Laddie was beginning to respond to some of the simple commands like "mush," "hike," "come gee," "come haw," and "whoa."

After several days of training, Ty decided to follow the path the other dogs had made into the woods. He thought Laddie was ready for a longer run. Besides, Ty was curious about how it would feel to run through the dark woods, between the trees, on a narrow path. It seemed spooky and mysterious.

The trail in the woods was packed down firmly, so the sled moved easily over the snow. Laddie ran happily through the dark woods at a brisk pace, while Ty ran behind the sled.

Ty soon became tired, so he stopped the sled and got onto it. "Mush! Hike!" he shouted.

Using all his strength, Laddie pulled the boy and sled through the woods at a much slower pace than they had been going. Ty was enjoying the ride. He trusted Laddie to stay on the trail.

Suddenly, out of nowhere, a large bull moose appeared on the trail. He stood like a statue, firmly planted across the sled path.

Laddie stopped dead in his tracks. He didn't even bark. The old dog was totally paralyzed by the huge animal standing about fifty yards in front of him.

Ty sat frozen in the sled. Even the forest was quietly anticipating what the bull moose would do next.

The bull put is head down to charge. Suddenly, a large, black wolf appeared out of nowhere and circled the moose. The bull stood for a moment, curiously eyeing the wolf while considering his next move. The moose raised up on his hind legs as the wolf began running circles around him.

The wolf circling the moose

The wolf crouched down, slowly circling, getting ready to spring at any moment. Then it leapt at the hind legs of the moose, nipping at his heels and slashing at the bull's hindquarters. The moose bellowed at times, and the wolf growled. As the wolf leaped into the air a third time to attack, the moose gave a mighty kick with his right hind leg and caught the wolf on his front right shoulder. The wolf fell backward into the snow.

The moose whirled around to strike the wolf with his huge antlers. The wolf recovered from his fall and danced out of the way as the antlers swept past him.

The moose stood silently for a few seconds, and then he turned and ran into the woods, making a loud bellowing sound.

The forest became eerily quiet.

The wolf stood silently glaring at the boy and the old dog. No one moved.

Ty's heart skipped a beat. *Oh, my God*, he thought. *Now he's going to eat us.*

Laddie lay down in the snow and whimpered softly. The wolf walked over to Laddie and sniffed him.

Next Laddie rolled over on his back—submissively—to show the wolf he didn't want to fight.

Ty sat in the sled—petrified—waiting for the wolf to attack the dog. The wolf sniffed Laddie for a second time, then turned and walked into the woods, disappearing into a dense thicket.

It took Ty a few minutes to clear his head and get up the courage to get out of the sled and see how Laddie was doing. The old dog remained on his back in the snow.

"Are you okay?" Ty asked the dog.

Laddie rolled over and stood up. He gave a sharp bark and pulled on the sled.

"Okay, boy, let's go home," Ty said while petting the dog between his ears. "You were very brave standing up to that wolf like you did. You'll get a special treat when we get home."

Ty helped Laddie turn the sled around, and Laddie took off for home at full speed, with Ty running behind the sled as fast as he could go.

* * *

"Oh, come on! You guys are so lazy!" Audrey scolded Jenny and Missy. "Skiing is fun and good exercise. All you want to do is lie around here and play computer games!"

"I'm tired," Jenny complained. "We were out exercising the dogs all morning. Give us a break!"

"I suppose we could try for a little while," Missy said meekly.

"That's the spirit," Audrey smiled. "Let's get some skis from Hannah."

"Oh, all right," Jenny moaned. "Don't ever say I didn't do anything you wanted to do. I'll remember this the next time I want to do something and you don't."

"Yeah, sure!" Audrey mumbled as she headed for the shed to get out all her warm skiing clothes.

* * *

Audrey instructed her two friends on how to ski in the same manner that Hannah had instructed her. She told them about the makeup of the cross-country skis as they each attached a pair to their ski boots.

The lessons took a turn for the worse when Jenny and Missy tried to follow Audrey by moving one arm at a time with the opposite leg. Both girls fell down into the snow, laughing.

"You two are so lame!" Audrey said, taking a deep breath. "Come on—watch me—glide like this." Audrey demonstrated again.

After some practice, all three girls were gliding around in a circle, with Audrey in the lead.

"Good job," Audrey said. "Now, let's get some poles and learn how to use them."

After Jenny and Missy had finally mastered the basics, the group set off down the ski trail.

Audrey kept shouting, "Stride, reach, glide," as they crossed the lake and headed into the woods.

They hadn't gone more than a few city blocks when they saw Ty and Laddie coming lickety-split down the trail toward them.

"Go back—go back!" Ty gasped exhaustedly as he and Laddie approached the girls.

Audrey grabbed her little brother as Laddie and the sled swept by her. They fell together into the snow beside the trail.

"What happened?" Audrey asked, holding her tired, trembling little brother in her arms.

"A big moose tried to attack us," Ty gasped while trying to catch his breath. "A big black wolf came out of the woods and chased away the moose, and then he looked like he was going to eat us."

"My God!" Audrey said. "What happened next?"

"Laddie saved us. When the wolf tried to eat him, he lay down and pretended to be dead, and the wolf left," Ty said proudly.

"I'll bet he was scared to death!" Jenny scoffed.

"No," Ty insisted. "He was brave and knew how to fool the wolf."

"I'll bet that wolf was Chico," Audrey speculated.

"Let's go home," Missy suggested. "I've had enough skiing for one day."

"Good idea," Audrey agreed. *It's a good thing Chico is out there protecting all us dumb kids,* she thought.

Chapter 17

The Big Race

The rules for the race were simple: (1) A sled can have seven to nine dogs; (2) there can be no more than two mushers per sled; (3) The race is eighty miles long between Moose River Bend and Willow city; (4) The first contestant to cross the finish line wins; and (5) There is one stop at Beaver Tail Lodge, where dogs and drivers can rest and eat for one hour.

The whole family accompanied Hannah and Basil to Moose River Bend the morning of the race. They had gotten up early, because the race started at 9:00 a.m. The children slept in the van along the way. Laddie was in the van with the children and grandparents, while Hannah and Basil had put the sled in the back of their pickup and the dogs into a covered trailer they pulled behind the pickup.

When the group arrived at their destination, there were many sleds, dogs, and mushers already set up and ready to go.

"We'll have to hurry to get organized," Hannah said as the children excitedly spilled out of the van.

Everyone knew their jobs. Hannah had organized the project the night before. She started barking her orders like an army drill sergeant, while Basil and Grandpa took the sled out of the trailer.

"You girls put the booties on the dogs," Hannah commanded, "and you boys put the harnesses on. Abby, Ty, and I will hold the dogs until Josh and Basil get the sled ready."

Everyone sprang into action.

The dogs and sleds were all set up in close proximity, so the other mushers were watching the Husky Hideaway entry getting set up. Ralph Redlin's dog team was set up next to Basil's team.

"Nice to see you made it," Ralph said to Basil. "I like some good competition when I'm racing." Ralph put emphasis on the word *good*.

"So do I," Basil replied. "I hope the weather stays nice so we can have a good race."

"The TV weatherman said we might get a little snow later this afternoon, around the time we all get to Willow City," Ralph volunteered.

"Sounds good," Basil said and then added, "I'd better keep an eye on my crew so they don't get this team hitched up backward."

Ralph chuckled. "Seems like you've got plenty of help."

"Too much at times," Basil said, and he laughed. "Well, good luck—see you on the trail."

Ralph nodded and walked away.

* * *

Some of the musher's were feeding their dogs raw meat before the race began. A man with a large hooded parka and sunglasses on was giving Ralph's nine dogs some fresh rabbit meat.

Basil's dogs saw the meat and began to bark. The man in the parka threw a large piece of rabbit meat to Stella. The dog grabbed the meat and gobbled it down.

Randy and Denny saw the man give Stella the meat.

"Stop that!" Randy cried. "We feed our own dogs."

"Yeah," Denny chimed in. "Mind your own business."

"He could overfeed our dogs and make them sluggish," Randy whispered to Denny. "We need them to be a lean, mean, running machine."

"Right!" Denny laughed and gave Randy a high five.

The man in the parka grabbed his pail and left.

*   *   *

The race judges were walking around to each team and giving the mushers last-minute instructions.

The girls were giving the dogs hugs and words of encouragement.

"You be really smart today, Buster," Audrey said as she hugged the team's lead dog. "You do everything right, and lead this team to victory. Remember that Hannah and Basil need that money to save the lodge."

Buster wagged his tail and licked Audrey's face. He was excited to get going.

Jenny and Missy went down the row of dogs. First they hugged Eddy and Andy, the swing dogs, and told the dogs they would get a special treat if they won. Neither girl knew what the treat would be, but they both knew that Hannah would have special treats for them all when they got home from the race.

Jenny moved to hug Mabel and pet her on the head. She also scratched Mabel behind her ears. Mabel loved the attention and barked happily.

Missy sat down beside Stella, who was lying in the snow. "Come on, girl—you're not tired—today's a big day! Get up!"

Stella lay quietly in the snow, and then she whimpered.

"Get up," Missy pleaded. "Please get up."

Stella lay quietly and closed her eyes.

Missy got up and ran to Basil, who was visiting with some other mushers. "Something is wrong with Stella," Missy said with tears in her eyes. "She won't stand up."

Basil ran to the dog and whispered, "What's wrong, Stella girl—are you tired?"

The dog opened her eyes and whimpered. Basil unhitched Stella from the sled, picked her up, and ran to the van where the local veterinarian was sitting waiting for the race to start. Doc Martin was always present at the dog races to make sure all the dogs were healthy and not abused during the race.

The doctor took a quick look at Stella and said, "What's she been eating? Looks like she's got a tummy ache."

"Nothing," Basil said. "I haven't fed my dogs since early this morning. I won't feed them again until I get to Beaver Tail Lodge."

The children, grandparents, and Hannah were all standing around the van and overheard the conversation between Basil and Doc Martin.

"Some guy fed Stella a big piece of meat about ten minutes ago," Denny said.

"What guy?" Basil wanted to know.

"Some guy in a parka and sunglasses," Denny replied.

"Where is he?" Basil asked.

"I don't know." Denny shrugged his shoulders.

"You kids go find him. I want to ask him some questions," Doc Martin said.

The children ran helter-skelter in all directions to look for the man in the parka and sunglasses.

"We'll have to pump her stomach right now," Doc Martin said. "I'll take her to my office right away. This dog won't race today."

"You go with Stella and the doctor," Basil told Hannah. "I have to get the team started. The race is ready to begin. I also have to get another dog."

"How are you going to race and get another dog at the same time?" Hannah shouted out the window, as the doctor's van took off with the tires screeching on the pavement.

Grandma and Grandpa stood looking at Basil with questions written all over their faces.

"Why don't you race, and I'll go get the dog?" Grandpa suggested.

"That wouldn't work. I'm too heavy. We've got one dog less, and my weight will slow the team down. We need someone that weighs less to drive the team."

Basil paused a moment to think. "I guess the boys will have to take the team out. They can handle it," he said. "They are good mushers. We'll find them and get them started; then Josh and I will get another dog. Abby, you'll have to drive your van, the supplies, and the other kids to Beaver Tail Lodge."

The adults saw the boys running around the streets looking for the mystery man.

"Come here!" Basil shouted while waving frantically to the boys. "I need your help!"

Randy and Denny came running at full speed.

"You're going to have to take this sled and dogs on the race. I have to get another dog."

"B-but," Denny stuttered. "We've never been in a race before!"

"There's a first time for everything," Basil said. "I know you can do this."

"We can do this, buddy," Randy patted Denny on the back. "It's a piece of cake."

"W-where will we go?" Denny stammered. "We don't know the trail."

"Just follow the others," Basil said. "It's going to be daylight while you race, so you can see their tracks. Try to keep up with them, and then you can see them all the time. That's all I'm asking you to do."

"That's all!" Denny gulped. "That seems like a lot."

"You'll have to take turns running behind—only one in the sled at a time. We're short a dog, so we have to lighten the load if we want to keep up with the other sleds. I'll meet you halfway, at the Beaver Tail Lodge. I'll have another dog to hitch up there. Then I can take over. I can't run forty miles behind that sled to keep the weight down; you two guys weigh a lot less than I do."

Basil could see the frightened look on Denny's face. He put his arms around Denny and Randy and said, "You'll be fine. I have faith in you. I'll meet you at Beaver Tail Lodge and we'll hitch up a new, fresh dog. The rest of the family will bring the van with the food, so we can feed and water the dogs. Now, go on over to the sled and give the dogs a pep talk. I need to get going."

With that said, Basil got into the pickup with Grandpa and took off, leaving Denny standing in shock, his mouth hanging open.

Randy had a big grin on his face. "Come on, buddy." He patted Denny on the back. "This is going to be a blast!"

The boys ran to the sled, settled the dogs down by talking to them, and checked all the equipment, harnesses, and sled.

"I'll take the first run," Randy said. "When I get tired, we'll switch."

Denny climbed into the sled.

There were ten teams, all lined up in a row. The guy with a start gun stood to the side of the teams and yelled, "Ready . . . Set . . ." and then he fired the gun.

The dogs took off like rabbits being chased by a wolf. The race was on.

Following the trail

Chapter 18

The Race Is On

The boys followed in the tracks made by the other mushers. Randy ran behind the sled and pushed it. When the sled was going downhill, Randy jumped onto the runners and took a ride. The boys managed to keep up with the other mushers. It was a clear day, and the temperature was ten degrees above zero. After about five miles, the dog teams began to slow down a bit. Randy stopped the team and switched places with Denny.

"Go get 'em," Randy yelled to Denny and the dogs as he jumped into the sled to rest.

Denny shouted, "Mush! Hike!" and the dogs jumped into action, led by Buster, who was anxious to get going again.

There was a heavily wooded area looming in the distance. The boys watched the other mushers disappear into the woods one by one.

"I hope we can find them in the woods," Denny said with uncertainty in his voice, as he lowered his head to talk to Randy in the sled.

"We'll follow the tracks if we lose them," Randy assured Denny. "I'll bet that Buster is a good tracking dog, and he'll know the way even if we don't."

Denny smiled with relief, but he still felt a little sick to his stomach. He was remembering the last time he and Randy had gotten lost in the woods.

The sled tracks took different paths through the woods. Denny wondered which one to take. Buster wanted to turn right and take that path.

"Should I let him take the lead?" Denny asked Randy.

"Why not? He can smell the other teams and probably knows where to go," Randy assured Denny.

The boys put their trust in Buster and let him take the lead as they went deeper and deeper into the woods.

Suddenly Buster stopped short. There was a drop in the trail. It looked like the sleds before them had suddenly dropped off an eight-foot-high embankment onto the trails below.

The boys walked in front of the sled and inspected the drop-off ahead.

"I-it looks steep," Denny stuttered.

"What do you think, Buster?" Randy bent over and asked the lead dog as he petted the animal on the head.

Buster barked and moved forward. It looked as if he wanted to go over the embankment. The tracks in the snow below showed that some of the sleds that had gone over the embankment had tipped over.

"You hold the sled down while the team and I go over this embankment," Randy said. "I'll go in front and lead them. We don't want the dogs to go too fast—that could tip us over and bend the sled. We don't want that to happen—it would slow us down."

"Good plan." Denny agreed.

Denny sat down in the snow behind the sled and took hold of the runners.

Randy grabbed Buster's harness. "Mush! Hike," he said in a calm voice to Buster.

Randy slid over the embankment, pulling Buster behind him. The other dogs followed, and then came the sled.

The sled started going over the embankment, with Denny hanging on for dear life. As the sled hit the bottom of the drop with a thud, Denny had to brace himself so he didn't land on top of the sled.

When everyone was safely at the bottom of the embankment, Denny and Randy burst out in hysterical laughter.

"What a blast that was!" Denny said, half laughing and half crying from relief as the tension flowed out of his body. "I thought I'd end up with a broken bone."

"You did great, buddy." Randy patted Denny on the back. "Get into the sled. I'll run for a while."

The team was off again, with Buster, in the lead, barking happily.

The forest suddenly ended and the boys saw a clearing ahead. They could see some of the other teams about a quarter of a mile ahead of them.

We need to catch up, Randy thought. "Tshckt, tshckt," he shouted to Buster, who leaped forward to pick up the pace.

"Faster, faster," Denny shouted. The sled sped through the snow. Soon the Husky Hideaway team was right on the heels of the last team.

"Go, boy," Randy shouted to Buster. Buster pulled the team slightly to the right and drove past the team ahead of him.

We'll stay in this position if we can, Randy thought. *Let the others break the trail.*

"Let's switch places," Denny shouted to Randy when they were a good distance ahead of the team they'd passed. "I'll run for a while."

Randy stopped the dogs, switched places with Denny, and they were off again at full speed.

The team next passed the halfway mark to Beaver Tail Lodge. There were about ten snowmobiles sitting along the side of the trail, with well-wishers cheering the mushers on. The boys waved as they sped past the snowmobiles and cheering people.

Randy and Denny switched places one more time before they spied another patch of forest ahead.

"Look," Denny said, pointing from the sled. "Another ugly forest."

"We'll be okay." Randy smiled while riding on the runners. "We made it through the first forest; we should be able to make it through this one too."

The trail through the forest became narrower as it became more tangled with trees, bushes, and thickets. There were large cliffs on either side of the trail. The other sleds had disappeared into the bowels of the forest. Randy slowed the team down. Buster ran cautiously, but at a steady pace. He was trying to follow the tracks left by the other teams.

The trail took a sharp turn to the left, where a large tree trunk lay across the road. The cliffs and thick growth of greenery on either side of the path made it impossible to get around the fallen trunk.

"How did that get there?" Denny asked.

"Somebody put it there to slow us down." Randy pointed toward the trunk. "See the footprints around the tree truck?"

"What a dirty trick!"

"Yeah. Come on, Denny, let's try to move this thing."

The boys tugged and pulled with all their might but couldn't move the trunk.

"We could go back a ways, where the forest wasn't so thick, and see if we can find another path," Denny suggested.

"That would waste too much time, and we might get lost," Randy surmised. "We'll have to unhitch the dogs and hook them up to this trunk to help us."

"Yeah, I guess so. That will delay us too, but it's probably the only way we can move this trunk."

The boys worked as quickly as possible, untying the team and hooking it onto the trunk of the tree. When the team was ready, Randy shouted, "Mush! Hike!" The dogs and boys all pulled at once, and the trunk moved a few feet.

"That's going to work," Denny said. "If we can just move the trunk a few more feet, we can sneak by on the right side without getting the sled hung up in the tree branches."

"Mush! Hike!" Randy shouted again. The group gave a mighty pull, and the trunk began to move slowly to the left. The group pulled with all their strength until the path was cleared. Then they hooked the team back onto the sled, and the group was off, winding their way through the forest.

* * *

"We must be getting close to Beaver Tail Lodge," Denny shouted when they spotted the other teams ahead of them as they exited the thick forest. The team they had passed seemed to have disappeared. Maybe they got lost.

Denny looked at his wristwatch. "It's almost one o'clock. We've been on the trail for about four hours. I'm getting hungry."

"Me too!" Randy gasped while running and panting. "But we should try to catch the other teams before we get to the lodge."

The boys put on a last-minute push. They sped through the snow until they could see the tall ski lodge, nestled on the side of a high hill, coming into view.

The lodge was a three-story Tudor-style building that covered a city block. It contained a restaurant, a bar, a hundred sleeping units, a recreation room, an entrance lounge, and an exercise room. Next to the lodge was a large parking lot, surrounded by storage sheds and a variety of other buildings. There were also some trailer homes nearby, where the workers and the boss lived.

"Let's switch places," Denny suggested. "I'm rested. I'll give it a good push the last half mile or so."

The boys quickly changed places. Buster could smell the other teams, so he was very excited about catching up. He also seemed to know there would be food when they got to Beaver Tail Lodge. Buster had run this race many times before.

When the teams entered the lodge area, they saw crowds of people standing along the road, cheering them on. The Husky Hideaway team crossed the halfway marker in eighth place, just a few minutes behind the lead team. Two teams had disappeared in the woods. The boys and dogs were very hungry and tired.

* * *

Grandma and the other children were waiting in the crowd. They ran over to the boys with the team and congratulated them on their first try at being racing mushers.

"You boys did just great!" Grandma said, giving them each a big hug. "I'm so proud of you. Grandpa and Basil aren't here yet, but I'm sure they will be coming soon."

"You guys were awesome," Audrey said. "I'll bet you had a blast!"

"Yeah," Randy said, grinning, "it was a real blast."

Denny grinned as well. He was too tired to care about any compliments. All he wanted to do was eat and rest.

The girls hugged and petted the dogs while they fed them scraps of meat. Grandma fed the boys some warm soup and sandwiches.

Ty sat down in the snow and ate with the boys. He liked to hang out with the big guys.

"You were wonderful," Audrey said to Buster as she handed him a scrap of raw meat. "You all did so well. I'm so proud of you." She petted the big dog as he ate his lunch.

Missy and Jenny fed the rest of the dogs, while Laddie sat in the snow, watching.

After they'd finished eating and feeding the dogs, Grandma suggested the boys go into the lodge and get warmed up. Just then, Basil, Hannah, and Grandpa drove up in the old pickup, with Babe tied in the back.

Everyone began talking at once, trying to fill the newcomers in on the events of the morning racing.

"Hold on!" Basil shouted over the noise. "One at a time. Randy, you go first."

Randy related the happenings along the trail, with some input from Denny.

"That Ralph!" Basil exclaimed. "He'll do anything to win this race. We'll show him, won't we, team?"

Everyone jumped up and down and cheered at the same time. Even Grandma and Grandpa did a few hip, hip, hurrahs.

"Why did you bring Babe?" Ty asked after the shouting had subsided.

"Because she is an experienced racer and a good one," Basil answered. Then he continued, "I didn't want to bring her at first, because she's out of shape from having the puppies and raising them, but I have no choice now. None of the other dogs have been fully trained to race. We can't put an inexperienced dog on the team—that could be a disaster."

"You've got about half an hour before you leave again," Grandma said to Basil. "Have some lunch and relax. It's still forty miles to the finish line."

"Thanks, I will." Basil chuckled. "I can't eat too much; I don't want to put on any more weight!"

The group got a full report on Stella from Hannah. The vet had found a piece of half-digested poisoned meat in her stomach when he'd pumped it empty. Stella would be okay after a few days' rest.

At 2:00 p.m. sharp the teams lined up and took off in the same order they had come into the halfway arena. Basil's team was ten minutes behind the lead team. He had some time to make up.

Chapter 19

Willow City or Bust

"Why don't we look for the guy who fed Stella the poisoned meat?" Jenny asked.

"There are lots of guys walking around with hooded parkas and sunglasses," Audrey answered.

"That guy was young and skinny. Most of the men around here are older and pretty heavyset," Randy added to the conversation.

"Let's spread out in teams of two," Jenny suggested. "Look for anything that might be suspicious. We could ask some of the spectators if they saw something."

"Good plan," Denny agreed. "Let's go. We'll have to head out to Willow City soon. We want to be there for the end of the race."

Audrey and Ty went into the restaurant at the lodge. They spied a waitress who was taking a break at a corner table.

"Excuse me," Audrey said politely. "We're looking for a friend. He's tall and thin and wearing a hooded parka and sunglasses."

"Lots of tall, thin, hooded parkas walking around today," the waitress said in a nonchalant voice.

"This guy's name is Mason," Audrey added.

"Oh yeah," the waitress piped up. "I know Mason Moses. He's kind of creepy. He was in here a few minutes ago—right after the sled racers came in. He left when the sleds left."

"If you see him, don't tell him we're looking for him," Audrey said. "We want to surprise him."

"Okay," the waitress answered while taking another sip of her coffee.

*   *   *

Jenny and Missy stealthily snuck around the back of the lodge. Jenny could hear voices by the woodpile near the back door. She stopped in her tracks and turned to look at Missy, who was right behind her. She put her right index finger up to her mouth and whispered a soft *shhhh* to Missy.

The girls crept closer to the woodpile and listened.

"I think we've got this race in the bag—if we can get Basil's team off track," the low raspy voice of a man said. Then he coughed.

Sounds like he's a smoker, Jenny thought. *That was a smoker's cough and voice if I ever heard one.* Jenny had a friend in Sioux Falls whose father smoked all the time and sounded like that.

A younger-sounding voice, sluggish and thick, answered, "Awesome, dude! I'll snowmobile ahead and set up the trap by Rocky Creek, about ten miles out of Willow City. We'll have to wait until Ralph and his team have gone beyond that point. This is going to be so cool."

"Good," the smoker answered. "See you in Willow City."

The smoker started walking toward the back door of the lodge. Jenny and Missy froze—holding their breaths and hoping he wouldn't turn around.

Dear God, Missy prayed silently, *don't let them catch us.*

The smoker went right in through the back door of the lodge without looking around.

The girls stayed crouched down in two little balls near the woodpile, waiting to see what the last man would do.

After a few seconds, the last man started a snowmobile, got up on the seat, and took off.

Jenny peeked out from behind the woodpile and read the license plate on the snowmobile. "Number XL280" she said to Missy. Then she repeated, "Number XL280—remember that. We'll have to give that number to the sheriff."

* * *

"I don't see anyone that looks like the guy we saw feeding Stella the poison meat," Denny said in dismay. "He's probably hiding someplace."

"Yeah," Randy replied. "I'd be hiding too if I'd done something that mean."

Denny grimaced. "Me too," he said.

The boys saw Missy and Jenny running out from behind the lodge.

"Over here," Denny called.

"Guess what?" Jenny asked breathlessly.

"What?" Randy said.

"We saw two guys talking behind the lodge. They were planning to set up a trap about ten miles out of Willow City near Rocky Creek. We've got to warn Basil."

Audrey and Ty came out of the front door of the lodge and joined the group.

"What's up?' Audrey asked when she saw Missy. "You look like you've seen a ghost."

"We saw two men plotting a trap for Basil and the team," Missy said softly; there was worry written all over her face.

"We've got to tell Basil," Jenny said excitedly.

"We've also got to tell the sheriff," Audrey said firmly. "If those men are up to some more dirty tricks, they could be dangerous."

"Did you see who the men were?" Audrey asked.

"No, but one was a smoker and the other one was younger," Jenny answered.

"How do you know he was younger?" Audrey asked suspiciously.

"Because his voice and speech were different than an old person's," Jenny answered with a glare.

"I wonder if the young man was Mason," Audrey mused. "The waitress inside said she'd seen him here about ten minutes ago."

"I've never seen Mason up close!" Jenny said. She looked around the group. "Has anyone here ever seen Mason up close?"

"Yes," Audrey replied. "I got a good look at him when he was at the Husky Hideaway apologizing to Basil for stealing the puppy. I think I'd be able to recognize him if I saw him again."

"Hannah knows what he looks like," Denny piped up. "She and Basil have talked to him and Jeb many times."

"Let's find Grandma and Hannah and tell them what we've learned," Jenny suggested.

The children ran off toward the parking lot next to the lodge, where they'd last seen the van and pickup sitting.

* * *

Grandma and Hannah had finished putting everything back into the vehicles. They were sitting inside the van, talking and waiting for the children to return.

"Were have you kids been?" Grandma scolded. "We've got to get going."

The children relayed all they had learned to the two adults.

"We'll find the sheriff and tell him everything," Grandma said. "This is getting too dangerous for you kids to take care of. Those men could be desperate and do something foolish. I don't want any of you to get hurt."

The group found Sheriff Miller sitting in his van visiting with his deputy, Jeff Nelson. After telling their stories, the children waited breathlessly for the sheriff to say something.

"Good work, kids," Sheriff Miller complimented the group. "Now, can anyone tell me the license number on that snowmobile, so we can trace the owner and stop him before he commits a crime?"

Everyone looked at Jenny and Missy.

"I-I don't remember," Jenny stammered. "It was XL something. Do you remember Missy?"

"Yes." Missy smiled. "XL280."

"Good work, girls. I'll get right on this, and we'll stop that guy from causing any trouble. I'll need a description of both guys, so hang around a little while."

The sheriff's deputy got on his cell phone and called the office, while the sheriff wrote down the descriptions that Jenny and Missy gave of the two men they had listened to behind the woodpile.

Hannah, Grandma, and the other children walked back to the parking lot and waited for Jenny and Missy. When the girls arrived, Hannah made a suggestion: "Denny and Randy can come with me. The girls can go with Abby. I'll lead, because I know the way to the Johnsons' farm, the halfway point to Willow City. All the mushers will stop there for a break before doing the final stretch of the race. We'll tell Basil what we've learned when we get there."

*   *   *

Basil's team was succeeding in keeping up with the other teams.

I'll have to take a shortcut if I want to win this race, Basil thought. *I can cut off four miles if I go over that large hill ahead instead of around it. If I help push the sled up the hill, the dogs will make good time and be able to handle the last stretch going down the hill.*

Basil stopped his team to rest until the other teams were out of sight, and then he headed out over the top of Johnsons' Hill, which would bring him to Johnsons' Farm, the halfway point to Willow City.

Basil pushed the sled up the hill while Buster blazed a trail. Going down the hill was easier. Basil stood on the runners, and the sled moved quickly down the steep hill.

To everyone's surprise, Basil was the first to arrive at Johnsons' farm. They had heard via cell phones that Basil was behind the rest.

"Welcome," Farmer Johnson greeted Basil. "Surprised to see you in the lead."

"I took a shortcut," Basil said. "I'm just going to give the dogs a short rest and drink of water, and then I'm on my way. I want to get a head start, because my team isn't the strongest one in the race. We need to be far enough ahead so the others don't catch up to us the last twenty miles. I'd appreciate it if you'd let the rest of the mushers think I'm behind them."

Farmer Johnson shook his head and smiled. He liked Basil and wanted him to win the race. Farmer Johnson liked rooting for the underdog.

By the time the pickup and van arrived at the Johnson farm, Basil was gone.

"Oh dear," Hannah wailed. "We'll have to hope the sheriff stops Mason before he can do harm to Basil and the other racing teams."

* * *

The sheriff and his deputy got to Rocky Creek ahead of Mason. They had called their office and discovered that the snowmobile with the XL280 license plate belonged to Jebediah Moses. They knew the old man wouldn't be out causing trouble, so they assumed it must be Mason who was up to no good.

They hid the van behind some tall bushes and sat quietly inside it, near the creek, waiting for the snowmobile to make its appearance.

"I hear something," Deputy Nelson announced.

"Shhhh," the sheriff cautioned him.

A snowmobile came into view. The driver was following the creek bed. He stopped near the bridge, where he knew the dogsleds would cross the creek. He surveyed the area and then he drove his snowmobile behind a heavy growth of thickets. Mason got off his snowmobile and opened the seat to remove something.

The sheriff and deputy jumped out from behind the bushes. "Stop!" the sheriff shouted. "You're under arrest for vandalism."

Mason dropped the large bag he had in his hand and took off, running at full speed into the nearby woods. Deputy Nelson took off in hot pursuit.

Sheriff Miller opened the bag and found it full of sharp pieces of glass.

That's what he was up to, the sheriff said to himself. *He was going to scatter this glass in the snow near the bridge and cut the feet of the dogs that stepped in it.*

The sheriff put the bag of evidence into his van and waited for his deputy to return with Mason. After fifteen minutes the deputy returned, but he didn't have Mason with him.

"He got away!" Deputy Nelson said, hanging his head.

"That's okay," Sheriff Miller said. "He'll head for Willow City, and we'll grab him there. Get in—we'd better hurry!"

*   *   *

Fifteen minutes after Basil took off on the last leg of his journey, the other teams started arriving at Johnsons' farm. Each musher rested and watered his dogs and then took off at full speed. They all knew they would have to put out all they could the last twenty miles in order to win.

With the forest behind him, Basil let the dogs run as fast as they could go. Buster knew they were coming to the end of the race and he'd get fed a special treat, so he ran as fast as he could. The other dogs followed their leader.

Basil was getting very tired. He ran behind the sled as much as he could, but he had to jump inside once in a while to rest.

This slowed the team down, but he couldn't help it—he was no longer a young man, and running long distances tired him out.

Soon Basil could see the other sleds behind him. He knew they could see him too. The last two miles were on a downhill slant, so Basil stopped the team for their final rest. He walked up to Buster and petted the big dog on his head. "It's up to you, boy," he said. "I'm pooped. You'll have to win this race."

Buster seemed to understand as he looked into his tired master's eyes. Buster barked happily as if to say, "Let's go!"

Basil got into the sled and shouted, "Mush! Hike!" The team was off at full speed.

* * *

The eight dogsled teams that were left in the race entered the town of Willow City in close proximity. They were all within a few city blocks of each other.

Basil was still in the lead, but by only a few hundred yards. "Tshckt, Tshckt!" he shouted to the team.

Ralph's team kept getting closer, and now the finish line was a hundred yard ahead. Ralph was yelling at his dogs, "Hike, Hike!"

Buster could feel the other team coming closer. Then he saw Black Jack, Ralph's lead dog, pulling up on his right side. Buster didn't like Black Jack. Buster put all his strength into the pull. He stretched out to his full length and stuck his head as far forward as he possibly could.

Both teams crossed the finish line. It was a photo finish. The judges would have to decide who had won.

Chapter 20

Who Won the Race?

"The Husky Hideaway won by a nose," the announcer shouted after a brief inspection of the photograph taken at the finish line.

The children, grandparents, and the Elliotts jumped up and down, screaming, hugging, and kissing each other. The children hugged and kissed all the dogs. Everyone was extremely excited.

Ralph came over to where the Husky Hideaway group was celebrating.

"It's not over," he snarled, showing his front teeth. "I'm going to contest this race. You used too many people, you switched dogs, and you took a shortcut. All those things are illegal."

Ralph stomped away to find the judges.

Ty shuddered. "He looks like a scary Halloween pumpkin when he's angry."

"What do you mean?" Audrey questioned her little brother.

"He's got a big tooth missing in front, just like a carved-out Halloween pumpkin," Ty answered.

"Yeah, just like that picture you drew for the sheriff of Bigfoot," Jenny commented. Then a light bulb went on in her head.

"Ralph is Bigfoot!" Jenny shouted, jumping up and down.

Missy joined her. "Ralph is Bigfoot; Ralph is Bigfoot," both girls shouted as they danced and jumped around in the snow.

"Settle down," Grandpa ordered the girls. "What are you talking about?"

"Remember the picture of Bigfoot that Ty drew for the sheriff? Well, Bigfoot's front tooth was missing, just like Ralph's," Jenny said proudly.

"Well, I'll be a monkey's uncle," Grandpa declared. "You're right—I remember that."

The children ran to find Sheriff Miller and tell him the news.

* * *

Denny and Randy went into the local Cenex gas station to use the bathroom. The bathroom was occupied, so they had to wait. After a while a young man exited.

Randy looked curiously at the young man as he passed, and then he called out, "Mason?"

The young man turned. When he recognized the boys, he started to run.

"Get him!" Denny shrieked as Mason exited the gas station with the boys in hot pursuit. Mason ran around the back of the station.

"You follow him," Randy motioned to Denny. "I'll go the other way."

Denny chased Mason around the building. Randy was waiting around the corner. When Mason turned the corner, Randy jumped out and tackled him. Mason struggled to get free. Denny jumped on top of Mason, and together the two boys brought him down and sat on top of him.

Some of the patrons from the gas station had witnessed the pursuit and came over to see what was going on.

"Get the sheriff," Randy ordered. "This guy has been up to no good all day and needs to be questioned."

It wasn't long until the sheriff showed up and took charge. "Thanks, boys," he said. "We've been looking for this guy all day."

Sheriff Miller turned to Deputy Nelson. "Take him away, Jeff, and book him. Ask him some questions about what has been going on here today." Then the sheriff turned to the curious crowd that had gathered and said, "We're arresting him for vandalism."

*   *   *

A half an hour after the race was over, the three judges on the racing committee met with Ralph, Basil, Doc Martin, Sheriff Miller, Deputy Nelson, and Mason. The group was seated around a large table in the back room of the local cafe.

"We're here to find out what happened during the race," the committee chairman said. "It seems some very strange things took place. Ralph Redlin claims that Basil did some illegal things to win the race. Ralph, you can speak first."

Ralph had calmed down a bit, when he saw the deputy and Mason come into the room. Ralph didn't know what Mason had told the deputy.

"I'm here to protest the winner of this race," Ralph began calmly. "The Husky Hideaway team had three drivers in all; they switched dogs in the middle of the race; and Basil took a shortcut to the Johnsons' farm."

"What do you say to those accusations, Basil?" the chairman asked.

"First of all," Basil began, "there were never more than two people driving that sled at a given time. The rules don't say anything about switching drivers—after all, any one of us could get sick or hurt along the way and a new driver would be needed."

"That's true," the chairman nodded. "Go on."

"Second," Basil continued, "I never switched dogs during the race. I had to replace one dog before the race began, because Mason—over there," Basil pointed to where Mason was sitting beside the deputy, "who works for Ralph, poisoned one of my dogs. Doc Martin can testify to that. We added the new dog at Beaver Tail Lodge. I had signed up with a seven-dog sled, and I never used more than seven dogs. We were handicapped the first forty miles, because we only had six dogs to run."

"He confessed," Sheriff Miller spoke up. "He has admitted working for Ralph and trying to stop Basil's team."

All three of the judges looked at Ralph and Mason with disgust.

"And last," Basil continued, answering Ralph's accusations, "I did take a shortcut over the hill to the Johnsons' farm, but there is nothing in the rules that says we all have to follow exactly the same path to get from Moose River Bend to Willow City."

"That's right," one of the committee piped up. "As long as you all start together at Moose River Bend, the first one to cross the finish line at Willow City wins."

The rest of the committee nodded their heads in agreement. The room became quiet. "Anything else to say?" the chairman asked Ralph.

"No." Ralph hung his head in shame.

"Let's vote," the chairman said, looking at the other committee members. "All in favor of accepting Basil's team as the official winner, say "I."

"I," the committee answered in unison.

"Meeting closed," the chairman declared. "Congratulations, Basil; you and your team did a great job in the face of adversity. You're the winner of this year's Northern Lights Sled Dog Race."

Basil stood up and thanked the judges. He left the room and entered the main restaurant, where all his family and friends were waiting anxiously for the results of the meeting.

Basil looked so serious that everyone's heart sank—then his face broke out in a big grin. "We won!" he exclaimed happily. The whole crowd broke out into cheers and clapping.

Basil smiled and left the restaurant. He found his dogs waiting in the parking lot, where they had been given their treats. Basil walked over to Buster, with tears in his eyes, and hugged the big dog. "Thanks, buddy, you saved the Husky Hideaway."

Ty petting Laddie

That evening the family gathered in front of the fireplace in the great room of the inn for a cup of hot chocolate before they went to bed. They discussed the events of the day.

"What's going to happen to Mason?" Audrey asked.

"The sheriff said he wouldn't get jail time if he went into a drug-treatment program. He'll probably get probation for a few years," Basil answered.

"How about Ralph?" Denny asked. "He was behind all this."

"He was part of it, but that guy, Chad Zaper, from the Great Lakes Lumber Mill, was the real instigator. He was paying Ralph to vandalize my inn so he could buy it. He was the real troublemaker. That description Jenny and Missy gave the sheriff of the older man by the woodpile fit Zaper to a T. The sheriff picked him up in the Willow City Bar after Mason confessed that he had been working with Ralph and Zaper to get our team out of the race. When the sheriff got all three conspirators together, they all confessed their parts in the crime—as well as trying to incriminate each other."

"Well, I'm just glad it's all over!" Hannah declared.

"Me too," Grandma agreed. "All this nonsense about a monster running around in the woods—what a lot of hooey!"

"And don't forget Chico," Randy said. "We owe him a lot. He saved all us boys from disaster."

"Ah yes." Basil sighed thoughtfully. "What do all of you think of releasing Delilah and her pups when spring comes, so they can all be together with Chico?"

"Yes," the children all shouted at once, while giving a big thumbs-up to Basil's suggestion.

The room got eerily quiet. Everyone was thinking about the events of the past seventeen days. Ty sat by the fireplace, petting Laddie. A tear ran down his cheek.

"What's wrong, sweetie?" Hannah asked.

"I-I'm sad," Ty stammered. "I don't want to go home. We had so much fun here."

"Well, then," Hannah said with a smile, "you'll all have to come back again next Christmas, so we can continue this winter fun."

"Yay," the children shouted as they sprang up to run to their rooms. Grandma and Grandpa looked at each other and sighed. Then a big smile crossed Grandpa's face. He had removed his hearing aid before the family gathering by the fireplace—he had known what was coming.

"What a bunch!" Basil exclaimed with a chuckle. "What a bunch!"

Chico and Delilah